The Peroxide Pomp

In This Series

That First Heady Burn

True Vermilion

The Dark Shill

A Stack of Sawbucks

The Hillside Roble

The Peroxide Pomp

The Incidental Twin

Brawl in Bardo

The Window-Shade Job

The Convenient Patsy

The Artisanal Grifter

Shrink in the Shadows

Project Chartreuse

From a Desert Playa

The Tired Canary

A Desperate Frame-up

Trail of the Blue Agave

The Saucer-Heads

The Peroxide Pomp

The Peroxide Pomp

George Bixley

Published by Dagmar Miura
Los Angeles
www.dagmarmiura.com

The Peroxide Pomp

First published 2018

ISBN: 978-1-942267-79-9

ONE

t was all lies, every number, every estimate. Slater was at his desk, hunched over his computer, working on a list of expenses. His business partner, Max, had hired an accountant who was also a lawyer, thinking she would know how to spin things to evade notice by the tax man. But first Slater had to make stuff up. As investigators they dealt mostly in cash, and had plenty of shady expenses that they couldn't really defend with paperwork, but he had to give O'Dowd something, as she was nagging them about the impending end of the year.

Well after business hours, the sewing factories in the building had gone quiet. Slater slumped back in his chair and rubbed his eyes, burning from staring at the screen. It didn't seem fair that he had to do this while Max was out on a case, doing real work.

A knock at the door made him sit up. Nobody ever came here unannounced, especially at night. Locking his computer with a keystroke, he stepped out of his cramped little office into the similarly meager outer office, pulling the door to Max's closed.

When he opened the front door he found a skinny pasty guy, with oily red hair and freckles, wearing a dark suit jacket over a black T-shirt. He looked like the floorwalker at an after-hours pool hall.

"What do you need, Stretch?" Slater said, looking him over.

"Max Conroy?"

"Who's asking?"

The redhead frowned. "Answer the question."

"Eat a dick," Slater said, and closed the door.

But the redhead had other ideas, shoving his foot inside to block it. Slater stepped on his shoe, shifting all his weight onto it. Wearing thin casual loafers, the guy felt it, yowling and pounding on the outside of the door frame.

"Get off me," he shouted.

Slater yanked the door open again and punched him in the face. His head snapped back, and he staggered away, clutching at his nose.

"If you're going to play tough guy, you ought

to wear tougher shoes," Slater said, following him into the hall. He stopped when he saw someone else out here, fleetingly thinking this might be an ambush. A tall figure, a woman, Latin, with dark hair, long and styled like she had time and money to spend on it. Not one of the laborers in the neighboring sewing factories, this was a woman of means, wearing a dark suit, gold jewelry visible at her collar, a pocketbook in hand, like she was going to the opera. She wasn't about to jump Slater.

The guy had stumbled farther down the hall, looking at his palm. "You broke my nose."

"I doubt that," Slater said.

"I'm bleeding," he snapped.

"What are you looking at, sister?" Slater demanded, turning to the woman.

"Are you Max Conroy?" she said. Her accent was subtle, but English was definitely not her first language.

"Are you with him?" Slater demanded, gesturing to the redhead.

She pursed her lips and glanced at him, standing there wiping his hands on a handkerchief.

"You need to teach your monkey some manners," Slater said, and seeing the guy look up to glare at him, added, "Don't try it—I'll flatten you."

The redhead huffed in frustration but didn't move.

"I can tell from here that your nose isn't broken, you big baby. Go put some ice on it."

"I ought to call the cops," he said.

"Go for it. You can explain why you forced your way into my office."

The woman said, "Randall, zip it. Nobody's calling the police."

Slater raised his eyebrows, eyeing the redhead. "Randall?"

Randall took a step toward him, and Slater balled his fists, ready to engage, but the woman stepped between them, facing Slater, her arm out to dissuade her companion.

"I'm sorry if Randall is overprotective," she said. "I sent him ahead to make sure it was safe, and that you were really here. Max, I need your help."

"I'm not Max," Slater said, "but I'll let him know some crazy people dropped by."

She dropped her chin then, and squeezed her eyes shut, her mouth tightening, her face contorted with emotion.

"Oh, Christ, don't do that," Slater said, and to Randall, "See what you've done?"

Randall just glared at him, murder in his eyes.

"Why don't you come inside and tell me about it," Slater said, and the woman looked up at him, recovering her composure a little too quickly.

"Randall, go wait in the car," she said, turning to him.

"It's not safe for you to be alone here."

"I'll be fine. Please go."

Randall scoffed and flipped his jacket tails, striding toward the elevator.

Slater held the door open for her, then closed it and locked the deadbolt. Stepping into his office, he waved at the chair in front of his desk. She glanced around as she stepped in, her brow furrowing. The place was pretty barebones, Slater had to admit, apart from the few pieces of rented furniture, the safe bolted to the floor in the corner, and a lone faded painting, three artichokes in a bowl, that Slater had found in a thrift store. Even he knew that didn't qualify as decorating.

"You always travel with a bodyguard?" Slater said, dropping into his chair. "He's not very good at it."

"He's more of a driver," she said, perching on the edge of the chair across from him and gesturing helplessly. "He volunteered to come up here with me. Your building is so run down, and the neighborhood is pretty rough."

"I guess it depends on your perspective. This is technically the Fashion District. In the daytime it's crawling with people who dress just like you."

"Your name was on the door with Max's," she said, and added something in Spanish. The only words he could parse were Ibáñez—his surname—and *"español."*

Slater spread his hands. "Sorry, *no comprendo.*" He had his father's dark Latin coloring, so people in Los Angeles, where half the population was Latin American, often made the assumption that he could speak Spanish.

She tilted her head, looking at him as if for the first time. "It's so strange to meet people who are so assimilated."

Slater frowned. "I wasn't assimilated. I was born here."

"Sure, but your people are from Mexico."

"They weren't. Half of them were from El Salvador." He studied her for a moment. "What's your name?"

"Marisol."

"Why do you need Max's help?"

"He's a PI. Are you too?"

"No, but we do the same kind of work."

"I'm not from here," she said, leaning back in the chair. "I don't know how to navigate your legal system."

"Where are you from?"

"Argentina," she said. "I married an American and came here six years ago. All my friends and family are in Buenos Aires."

He believed that, he decided. She was from a higher social class than most newcomers from

Latin America. But he wasn't buying the innocent shtick—six years was long enough to figure things out, and Buenos Aires wasn't exactly a backwater that fostered naïveté.

"Max isn't a lawyer. How is he going to help you with your legal problems?"

"I'm getting divorced, and my husband is harassing me," she said, her tone plaintive, her eyes growing wide. "I've come to be afraid of him."

Slater sighed. He hated this kind of work, boy-girl conflicts. "Have you talked to the police?"

"That's exactly what Abner wants—to make me look hysterical. That way he seems like the innocent party and I look combative and crazy. A judge has a lot of leeway about dividing assets. Going to the police to complain about him is just playing his game."

"Do you have a lawyer, at least?"

"Of course. But Liz said Max could talk to my husband without that conversation becoming part of the record, part of the divorce."

"Liz is one of Max's clients?"

"Max helped her prove that her husband was cheating."

That made sense—Slater avoided window-shade cases when he could, but they were Max's bread and butter. He'd worked for dozens of people like Liz, gathering evidence of furtive sex and romance for distrustful spouses, fiancés, newlyweds.

"I know my husband is cheating," Marisol continued, waving a hand for emphasis. "That's not the issue. I want him to stop the terror."

"What kind of terror?" Slater asked.

"He told everyone at our club that I cheated on him. The opposite is true, but it doesn't matter now what I say, because everyone believes it." She heaved a weary sigh. "The beautiful woman is always guilty in the court of gossip."

Slater nodded, frowning in mock sympathy.

"And he took my car. Abner had no right to do that. He brought it back when I threatened to report it stolen. I also know he's concealing assets, and moving money around."

"Those don't sound like reasons to be afraid of him."

"Well, he broke into my house—it used to be our house, but he moved out."

"Where's he living now?"

"I think he's in a long-term hotel by his office," she said. "I changed the locks, but he got in anyway. And he screams at me on the phone. He said, 'If I can't have you, no one will.'"

"That's definitely a threat," Slater said, leaning toward her. "The best thing you can do to protect yourself is go to the cops. File a report, then have your lawyer get a restraining order. That won't look unreasonable to a divorce judge."

"I told you, I can't go to the police," Marisol said, raising her voice, anger flashing in her eyes. As quickly as it boiled up, though, her face softened, and she dropped her chin. "Can't you help me?" she said, sticking out her lower lip, absently flipping back her hair, looking up at him.

It wasn't very often that Slater saw someone playing coquette. It probably worked better in Argentina. Here it just seemed exaggerated, an anachronism. And clearly she was mistaking him for straight.

"I can relay your request to Max," he said.

"Can't you do it?" Marisol said, straightening up.

"He's better at this kind of stuff."

"Is it about money?" Snapping open her pocketbook, she pulled out a sheaf of crisp new hundreds and set them on his desk, then met his gaze. "That's two thousand dollars. Is it enough to get started?"

Slater eyed the cash. It meant there was a lot of money at stake in the divorce, which made her problems a lot more interesting. "I think so," he said, and scooped up the bills, pocketing them. Pulling out his desk drawer, he found a notepad and flipped it to a clean page. "Tell me about your husband. What's his name?"

"Abner," she said.

"His last name?"

"Same as mine—Hart," she said, and spelled it. "He works as an accountant. In his own practice."

"Where's his office?"

"Koreatown. The Durham Building."

"Who filed for divorce?" Slater said, glancing up from his notes.

"Abner did." Her eyes welled up with tears, perhaps authentic this time. "He just threw me aside, like a sackful of trash on the side of the highway. I'm not trash."

"I know you're not," Slater said, and pulling out his phone, "Give me your number." He typed it as she recited it, then got to his feet. "I'll have a word with Abner."

"Thank you," she said, rising, relief in her expression. As she stepped into the front office, she turned back. "Just don't be fooled by Abner. He's charming, but he's tricky. A real snake."

Holding the door for her as she left, he stood there to listen for the rumble of the elevator coming to life, then, satisfied she was leaving, went back inside.

At his desk, he woke his computer and searched online for Abner Hart. The pages that came up were all mentions of his accounting practice, and the site for his business had a professional portrait of the guy, half-sitting on a desk in front of a bookcase, arms folded, looking at the camera and smiling. Part of a blotchy red modernist painting was visible behind his head. With the suit and the bottle-blond hair, he looked like an executroid, his expression wan and lifeless despite the fact that the photographer must have worked to make him not look that way. Fuckable, maybe, Slater thought, then read through the rest of the site.

The language that was used implied that Abner's services were high-end, with words like *prestigious*, and *blue-chip*, and *exclusive*. Farther down the page he hinted that he was also skilled at minimizing tax liability, like O'Dowd, the bean counter Max had put him in the thrall of, claiming his services were *confidential, knowledgeable, safe.*

In his pants Slater's phone buzzed, drawing his attention away as he pulled it out to check. It was a text from Andy, a guy he'd been sleeping with fairly regularly:

Coming over?

Slater thumb-typed a reply:

10 minutes.

The itemized expenses for O'Dowd were going to have to wait. Flicking off the room lights, he locked the office and took the elevator down to the street, jay-walking across to the surface lot where he parked his car. The classic '78 Thunderbird was one of the only vehicles in the lot, gleaming black in the semidarkness, waiting for him to climb in.

Starting the throaty engine, he pulled onto the street and drove the few blocks to Broadway, pulling into the lot behind Andy's building. Unlike where his office was, this neighborhood had nightlife, so the parking attendant was still here, and Slater paid him the flat evening rate.

Upstairs, Slater knocked on Andy's door. It took him a minute to answer, as he had some mobility problems from CP and moved slow, even using crutches when he was out on the street. When he finally pulled open the door, he was wearing boxer shorts and a sleeveless T-shirt. His thick brown hair was getting too long, a perfect tousled mess. Stepping inside, Slater put a hand on his bicep to stabilize him and leaned in to meet his mouth. At first Andy's random muscle movements had been a little disconcerting, but he'd figured out how to work with it.

Andy's space was a studio loft, mostly one big room, with a bed in one corner and a computer desk. The towers of the Financial District glittered in the darkness beyond the multipane windows, a holdover, along with the wooden floors, from when the building had been a warehouse.

"How's your tax prep going?" Andy said, leading him inside.

"I can't believe people actually do that. It's so boring it makes my brain hurt."

Andy turned back to him and ran his fingers through Slater's dark hair. "I wish I could … make it better."

"I know you can," Slater said, pulling him closer, his hands on his back.

"Let me undress you," Andy said softly.

Slater unbuttoned his shirt, and Andy pulled it off, breathing hard, then leaned in to kiss his chest, sloppy and warm and intent. Slater felt his dick swelling, and Andy sat on the end of the bed, then grappled with Slater's belt buckle, unbuttoning his jeans. Slater helped slide them down, and Andy kissed his belly. He wasn't about to let Andy blow him, with his lack of fine motor control, but there was lots of other stuff they could do.

Pulling off Andy's shirt and boxers, Slater lowered himself on top of him, letting his weight settle on his frame, which he knew turned Andy on. Andy ran his hands over Slater's back and his butt, and Slater reached for the bottle in the bedside table, lubing up and then thrusting between Andy's legs. It was a pattern they'd established that worked, and it was almost as good as being inside him. Pressing his belly against Andy's cock as he moved, he kissed him, kept their mouths tight together.

Andy's breathing tensed up. Slater could feel him getting closer, and pressed harder into him. Andy came, thrashing wildly, and Slater kept pumping a while longer until he came too, then buried his nose in Andy's sweaty hair. After the moment of shared intensity, as he caught his breath, he rolled onto his side, draping an arm across Andy's belly, still breathing in his hair. It was such a perfect scent, heat and sweat and soap.

Eventually Slater got up and grabbed a towel for them, and after Andy had tossed it on the floor, he stretched out with his head on Slater's chest.

"Did you work today?" Slater asked.

"A little, but I'm not very busy. Do you have something … for me?"

Andy did IT stuff remotely for private clients, and some of his skills had proven useful.

"If you have time. I picked up a case today."

"For your insurance company?" Andy said.

"It was a walk-in, which never happens. Maybe you can look into somebody." Slater meant he should hack the guy, although Andy never used that word, calling it instead "deep research."

"Sure—send me what you know about him."

Slater shifted position, folding his arm around Andy's shoulders, then closed his eyes. Just for a minute, he told himself, relishing the warmth of Andy's body.

———•———

Waking when Andy climbed out of bed, Slater sat up, shivering involuntarily. Andy kept it cold in here, as his metabolism revved high, his muscles constantly working, even when he wasn't doing anything. Slater stood up and pulled on his jeans.

"You can stay," Andy said, coming back from the bathroom.

"I have to go to my place."

"Call one of those delivery services. They'll bring you your stupid booze. You can get drunk here."

"That's not why I'm leaving."

Andy dropped onto the bed. "You don't have to lie to me."

"You don't want to see me when I'm winding down," Slater said, kneeling to tie his boots.

"That's such an odd … euphemism for getting shit-faced."

Slater paused to kiss him before he left.

Walking out to his car, Slater had to chuckle. Andy was a lot of fun, and he was easy to be around. The guy wasn't about to entertain any bullshit about what Slater was doing, but he wasn't judgmental either. That probably came from his twelve-stepping. Whatever the reason, he wasn't going to start sleeping there. Slater didn't need a freaking boyfriend. He'd made that mistake before.

Pulling into the alley behind his building in gritty Westlake, Slater nosed the Thunderbird into the garage, then waited for the heavy door to roll down. Having private space for his car was the best thing about this apartment, a rarity in a crowded neighborhood, and it kept him bound to the shabby one-bedroom, two flights up over a cell phone store. The kitchen was near the front door, and beyond was a living room with a thrift-store sofa and a worn recliner.

Waiting for him on the counter beside the fridge was a fifth of bourbon, patient and golden and gleaming. Cracking it open, he drank from the bottle, savoring the burn in his throat and then coughing from the intensity of it. The warmth started to hit his belly. He poured a tumbler full and dropped in an ice cube. In the dark, he stretched out on the sofa and sipped at the heady liquid, then set the tumbler on the carpet.

Marisol seemed so helpless, but that was almost certainly an act. Her money, however, was real. Sipping at the bourbon, he let go of it all—Marisol and her problems, the lawyer-accountant and that unfinished list of expenses—all of it receding. As his mind started to slow down, he turned on the radio, upbeat late-night house music, and slowly sank into it, feeling the world unspooling.

TWO

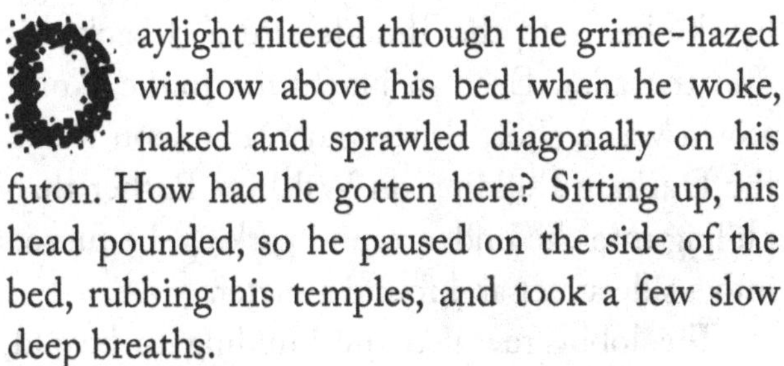

Daylight filtered through the grime-hazed window above his bed when he woke, naked and sprawled diagonally on his futon. How had he gotten here? Sitting up, his head pounded, so he paused on the side of the bed, rubbing his temples, and took a few slow deep breaths.

It was still morning, at least, he saw when he picked up his phone. Finally able to stand, he went into the kitchen and drank some water, then opened the fridge, barren except for a few jars and condiments. He pulled out the peanut butter and ate a spoonful, then munched on a pickle. Once he'd splashed cold water on his face, he started to feel awake, although his head still throbbed. His clothes were on the bedroom floor, and his jeans from yesterday were still presentable, but he put on a clean shirt.

"Thank you, Rosa," he said, realizing as he pulled it from the hanger that it had been ironed. A while back she must have gotten tired of working around his dirty clothes, because she'd taken it on herself to do his laundry, subsequently jacking up what she charged him. Clean clothes had turned out to be far more valuable than the futile labor of cleaning the place, with its ancient stained carpet, a decades-old fridge, the impenetrably grimy bathtub.

Trotting down the two flights to his garage, he climbed into the Thunderbird and backed it into the alley. Even in lunchtime traffic, Koreatown was a short drive, and Slater soon found the Durham Building on Wilshire. Rather than pulling into the underground parking, he turned into a side street and found a meter.

The lobby revealed the building to be old, maybe dating to the 1950s, but it was no classic. Slick utilitarian marble finished the walls, and the doors of the elevators were spare and modern. A uniformed security guard at the desk inside didn't look up when he walked in, the blue glow of the screen she was engrossed in illuminating her face. Scanning the directory on the wall, Slater found Abner's name and suite number. As he stepped away from it, the guard asked,

"Can I help you find someone?"

"I got it from the board," Slater said, and she looked down at her phone again as he walked back toward the elevators.

Upstairs, he found the door clearly marked:

ABNER HART
ACCOUNTANT

Twisting the handle and stepping inside, he found a small office, with a subtle security camera mounted high on a wall, pointed at the door. The green indicator below the lens implied that it was real. At the side sat a trio of chairs with a little table littered with glossy magazines, like a dentist's waiting room. Behind a desk sat a stout woman in a blue cardigan with wavy brown hair, her lips painted a dark shade of burgundy. Looking up at him through thick black-rimmed glasses, her brow furrowed as she gave him the once-over.

"Can I help you?"

Slater approached her desk and handed her his card. "I need to talk to Abner Hart."

Peering at it, she said, "You're selling insurance?"

"I'm not in sales," he snapped. "I'm having trouble itemizing my expenses."

"Are you a client?" she said, looking up at him again.

"Stop wasting my time," Slater demanded.

"Is he here or not?"

Keeping a wary eye on him, she lifted the phone and pressed a button with a carefully manicured fingernail, then said, "There's an insurance guy here to see you…. He says he's not selling anything. It's an accounting issue…." She replaced the receiver and nodded toward the chairs. "Have a seat."

Slater stood his ground, folding his arms and glaring at her. Turning back to her computer, she eyed him sidelong, clearly uncomfortable.

Before she could work up to saying anything else, the door to the back office swung open, and Abner stepped toward him, introducing himself in a nasal voice. That photographer really had spun straw into gold—in person he was more pallid and slighter than in his portrait, his shoulders hunched and rounded in a droopy green suit. His artificial blond hair was swept up into a pomp that didn't fit with his narrow face, making him look exaggerated, like a dandy, or a kid playing dress-up.

Slater told him his name and extended his hand. Abner's handshake was limp, and he pulled away too quickly, as if it were something he didn't do very often. Clearly Marisol had married this guy for the money, or for a green card—she was way out of his league.

"Come on in," Abner said, and pushed open the door.

This space was much bigger than the front office, with a broad desk, a credenza, and file cabinets, all in dark wood. This is where his portrait had been taken, in front of the bookcase. At one side was another door, with a deadbolt. On Abner's desk sat a few binders and a laptop computer, but there was no other tech, not even a printer, although he'd seen one of those in the front office, behind the receptionist. A lone laptop wouldn't be very useful for number-crunching, and overall the place was too tidy. This room was meant for show—the accounting work must happen elsewhere.

Abner stepped around behind his desk. Stretching along the wall above him was an oversize painting with three spotlights aimed at it. It was a horse, Slater decided, shaped like a contorted sausage, like something a preschooler would do, dark red, with tiny feet and a stringy tail. The whole thing was painted in shades of red, even the billowing clouds of the background.

"That looks expensive," Slater muttered.

Unlike the outer office, there was no security camera here. Slater watched the door they'd stepped through close itself with the hydraulic arm mounted at the top. The inside surface of the door was covered top to bottom with thick dark padding, and so was the side door.

"What goes on in here that you need soundproofing from your own staff?" Slater asked, gesturing to the door.

Abner grinned at him. "My clients appreciate the confidentiality." He waved to the chair in front of his desk. "Sit down."

Reclining in his chair, Abner laced his fingers behind his head, a gesture of confidence that didn't quite fit his spindly frame.

"You're in insurance?" Abner asked. "Are you an agent?"

"I'm not here about that," Slater said, holding his gaze. "I want to know what you hope to gain by harassing your wife. Are you just being a prick, or did you have a goal in mind? Maybe something about the division of assets?"

Abner laughed, unfazed. "Marisol thought hiring a thug would intimidate me? What she needs is a good lawyer, not a goon."

"You broke into her house," Slater said.

"That's my house."

"You don't live there anymore."

Abner sat forward, palms flat on the desk. "That's none of your business, cowboy. My advice to you is, don't get tangled up with her. She's trouble."

Slater eyed him for a moment. Abner ought to know; he'd married her. Why had he agreed to get enmeshed in this boy-girl baloney? But there was more to it, something about this guy. Abner had more going on than a regular civilian—he looked like a cream puff, but he had a hard edge, like he'd seen things get rough.

"She knows that you're already fucking someone else," Slater said.

Abner frowned. "What's it to you?" Then raising his voice, he added, "Are you sleeping with her?"

"Would it make any difference if I told you to stay away from her house?" Slater said.

"Get out," Abner snapped, his tranquil facade finally cracking.

Slater rose and stepped toward the door, then paused and turned back. "You know, I'm doing my year-end, and I'm still not sure what I can claim as business expenses. Can I deduct the rent on my apartment?"

"Who the fuck do you think you are?" Abner sputtered, his face red, rising from his chair.

Slater held up his palms in mock surrender. "You're right. I should talk to my own accountant. It's just that she's so damn expensive, and I figured you were kind of …" Slater glanced around the office, then met his eye: "cheap."

"Fuck you," Abner shouted.

Slater pulled open the door, walking out and ignoring the receptionist. It was simple to unnerve the guy—he was trying to look upscale and moneyed, so of course it would be upsetting to be told it wasn't working.

Stepping out, he walked in the direction oppo-site the elevators, following the hallway around a right angle. As he came to the next doorway, he stopped to think, working out the floor plan in his mind. Abner's private office had to be right here. This was the other padded door he'd seen inside his office—a back way into the hall.

Walking back around the corner, near the elevator lobby, there was a stepladder that hadn't been here before, spread open and with a guy in blue coveralls standing on it. One of the drop ceiling panels had been lifted out, and his head was half inside the dead space above. The logo on the back of his coveralls read WILLOWBROOK FIBER. A coil of blue wire from a box on the floor looped upward into the ceiling.

Slater stepped around the ladder, then paused, the flicker of an idea sparking in his mind.

"The internet is acting kind of spotty in my office," he said. "Is it something you did?"

The guy looked down at him and said firmly, "It's nothing to do with me. These cables aren't connected to anything yet."

"So what are they for?"

"Whatever the tenants want to pay for. Usu-ally fiber-optic internet—fiber has huge band-width. We're not a provider, though, so don't even ask. We just run the cables for the landlord."

"Are you going to be doing my office?" Slater said. "It's right around the corner."

He frowned. "We wired most of this floor already. I'm surprised you didn't see us."

"I've been away. So why are you putting it in the ceiling and not in the walls? Isn't there a utility conduit?"

"Doing this is a lot cheaper than pulling everything through conduit. Fiber has no voltage, so there's no danger—it doesn't need to be shielded."

"Who knew?" Slater said, eyeing the configuration of the drop ceiling and then walking to the elevator lobby.

When he got down to his car, there were still a few minutes left on the parking meter, so he sat and checked on his stupid cop ex-boyfriend, Conrad. The numbskull was at his station today, according to the location tracker on his phone. Slater had installed it surreptitiously back when they were still together. It didn't count as stalking, because he didn't really give a damn where the idiot was, but he needed his help sometimes. It was his own stupid fault for letting Slater see the code he used to access his phone.

He thumb-typed a text:

Are you around?

Slater already knew he was, and started the

Thunderbird's engine, pulling into the street and heading toward Rampart station, back in his own neighborhood. A few blocks later, Conrad's reply came:

I'm working.

Slater parked on the street out front and texted back:

Put your dick away and come outside.

There was no response, and Slater climbed out of the car, stretching and then wandering toward the building's front entrance. Soon Conrad came out, in his uniform, swarthy and barrel-chested, with that great black hair. Such a beautiful man.

Conrad waved him over to the accessibility ramp, away from the door, minimizing the possibility that a colleague might overhear them on the way past. The globe mallow bush in the bed along the ramp was blooming, a riot of orange flowers.

"What's with the golf shoes?" Slater said, looking at his feet. Conrad was wearing what looked like black sneakers with low heels.

"They're not golf shoes," Conrad said, frowning. "I needed to ditch the boots."

"I bought you those."

"They were getting ratty."

"So you bought golf shoes?" Slater demanded.

Conrad sighed. "Slater, what do you want?"

"I need you to run a records check on a couple of people. I'm not sure if they're dangerous or not."

Conrad furrowed his brow but nodded assent. Slater used to blackmail him into using police resources to help him out, but Conrad had admitted that he went along with it in an effort to keep Slater safe. Slater could take care of himself, and certainly didn't need this moron's paternalistic bullshit, but his resources were useful. All he had to do these days was frame the ask as if he might be in danger, which was a lot less work than bullying a cop. Slater wasn't afraid of Abner or Marisol, but Conrad was too stupid to know that.

"It's for an insurance gig?" Conrad said.

"A boy-girl divorce case. He's harassing her, and she's afraid of him."

"It sounds like she needs to come and talk to us."

"She's afraid of you too," Slater said. "I haven't figured out exactly what's going on yet. He definitely reads like a lowlife. I'm not sure about her. I need to know who I'm dealing with."

"Text me what you have on them." Conrad put his hands on his hips. "So who's the guy you've been seeing?"

"I'm not seeing any guy," Slater snapped.

"Doris said you had a regular squeeze."

"Never mind what Doris says. You need to quit talking to her."

"She said he lives in one of those lofts on Spring Street."

"It's on Broadway. And he's not my boyfriend—you managed to break me of that delusional aspiration."

Conrad winced at that.

Slater could feel his heart pounding. "Who are you fucking these days, besides your hand?"

Conrad shrugged. "It's hard to get close to people. You know how it is."

"I take that to mean any guy who's willing to schlep out to the ass-end of the Valley."

"There's lots of guys already in the Valley."

"Yeah, well, enjoy your golf game," Slater said, and turned to walk away.

"They're not golf shoes," Conrad protested.

"Say that as often as you want," Slater called over his shoulder. "It won't make it true."

When he climbed into his car and looked toward the entrance, Conrad was already gone. Such an infuriating idiot. Pulling out his phone, he texted him:

> Abner Hart, accountant, age maybe 50. Marisol Hart, from Argentina, looks 40 or 45.

Pulling into the traffic, Slater pushed thoughts of Conrad away, and drove through downtown to the Fashion District, at this time of day humming with activity. He parked in the surface lot across from his building, earning a wave from the parking attendant as he climbed out. None of them ever checked his pass after they'd done it once, as his classic ride was so readily recognizable.

Across the street, there was still a small crowd of day laborers in front of his building, waiting for gigs sewing or cutting or carting fabric and garments around for one of the factories, and he stepped past them into the lobby, then up to the ninth floor and around behind the elevator shaft.

As he twisted his key in the lock, he admired the raised lettering emblazoned on the door:

SLATER IBÁÑEZ
MAXIMILLIAN CONROY
INVESTIGATIONS

Max was in his office, reclining in his chair with his feet up on the desk. Beefy and with a gut that bulged over his belt, today Max was wearing a sharp gray suit, his yellow necktie loose at the collar, his holster strap visible under his jacket. His mousy brown hair looked better than it used to, trimmed and coiffed in a trendy style, making him look less like what he really was—the heavy. That had to be the influence of his girlfriend. Max set aside the sheaf of paper he was reading as Slater dropped into the chair in front of his desk.

"I have to confess something to you," Slater said.

"Is it bad?" Max said, eyeing him.

"You'll have to decide that."

"Unless you scratched my car or banged Vanessa, I'm not worried. And I know you didn't sleep with Vanessa, because she's not skanky and male."

Slater chuckled. "I poached a client who came up here looking for you last night." He explained what had happened, and Max confirmed that he had worked for a client named Liz on a window-shade job.

"Anyway, I'll split the fee with you," Slater said, and pulled out the wad of C-notes, shuffling through them and setting a grand on the desk.

"These look real," Max said, thumbing through the bills. "But I couldn't have taken the job right now. We work together, so it's not poaching."

"Even so, she was looking for you."

"I would have put her on to you anyway. Put this in the rent envelope."

"How about this," Slater said. "You take the grand, and if she pays me anything more, it's all mine."

"Deal," Max said, and tucked the bills into his pants pocket. "So did you look into the husband?"

"I met him this morning. He's this nebbishy accountant with a flashy office in Koreatown. Nobody would marry this guy except for his money."

"Don't let that lull you into complacency," Max said. "Sometimes those are the most dangerous people."

"All toxic under the schlubby facade?"

"More like boy-girl stuff makes people extremely irrational."

It was good advice, Slater thought, and went into his own office, waking his computer and checking his email. There was nothing from Conrad, that lazy ass. On the web he tried to dig up more on Abner, eventually finding himself scrolling through the guy's website. He'd already seen this. It didn't feel like he was accomplishing anything, and his head had been aching all day. He hadn't really eaten, he realized, and locked his computer, calling good-bye to Max and then heading down to the street.

There'd be a food truck around here somewhere, and he headed toward the boulevard, eventually locating one a few blocks away. At the window he ordered two avocado tacos.

It was getting easier to eat vegan at the bottom end of the economy, as people seemed to be getting used to the idea outside the wealthy Anglo enclaves. Even the women who made *pupusas* at home and sold them on the street were making a version with black beans and potatoes, which made Slater's life a lot easier.

The truck had a couple of plastic chairs set out

on the sidewalk, but he didn't need to be lounging around here, instead walking up the block and stopping to eat over the gutter, then pitching the wrappers in the trash, wiping his hands on his pants, and heading back toward his office. The long shadows from the low winter sun were encroaching on the city, depressingly early in the day at this time of year. His phone buzzed in his pocket, and he pulled it out. It was Marisol.

"I'd like to see you," she said, when he picked up.

"I haven't got much to report yet."

"There's new information that I'd like you to look into."

"Can you give it to me now?" Slater said.

"I'd rather meet. Can you come to my home?" She recited her address, and Slater stopped on the sidewalk to thumb-type it into his phone.

 THREE

B ack in front of his office, Slater crossed the street and climbed into the Thunderbird. The map on his phone showed that Marisol's house was in Los Feliz, up in the nice part near Griffith Park, and it sent him there on the 10 and the 5. That seemed counterintuitive, but he knew better by now than to second-guess the wisdom of the navigation software. Even if this was the fastest route, the evening traffic was sluggish.

Eventually he was driving up Marisol's winding hillside street. Most of these houses would have been mansions early in the last century, but today they were just nice houses on small lots. Marisol's address, incongruously, was a boxy new construction, rising at least four levels and towering over its neighbors. In front, looking out over the basin, it was all windows, the top floor the only part of the street that was still in sunlight. Built right to the property lines, it had to have gone up within the last few years, after the rules on density had been loosened.

Slater cruised slowly past, looking at the 1930s Tudors and midcentury bungalows farther along the block. By comparison, Marisol's house was an out-of-proportion monstrosity.

Pulling to the curb and killing the engine, Slater climbed out and walked back to the front door, pressing the bell. When she pulled it open, Marisol was dressed more casually than she had been last night, in a dark top and slacks, her hair pulled back, but still with the jewelry, several rings and a dangling silver necklace.

"Thanks for coming," she said, and Slater waited while she closed the door.

"Did you and Abner build this place?" he asked.

"Right after we were married."

"Your neighbors must hate you."

She frowned but didn't reply, leading him up a flight of polished wooden stairs, then down a hall and into a lounge. It was lined with dark wood and oversize leather furniture. A pair of stools fronted a small bar with shelves of bottles and a sink behind it.

French doors looked out on a miniscule yard, smaller than the room they were in, with a fence at one side and a concrete retaining wall holding up the hill. Despite the fact that there was just a sliver of sky, the space was heavily planted with ground-hugging foliage, succulents and local dryland poppies, and near the retaining wall, a manzanita. Slater wouldn't have put it there, but it was clearly thriving, and the yard looked well-tended.

"Are you the gardener?" Slater asked, gazing out at the space.

"We hire someone to take care of it," Marisol said, stepping behind the bar.

"At least the landscaping isn't suffering in the divorce. Do you leave those spotlights on all night?"

"The outside lights? I think they're on a timer. They switch off at midnight or something."

Slater turned to her. "You should turn them off unless you're using the yard. Plants need it to be dark at night."

Marisol frowned. "OK. Do you want a drink?"

"Bourbon or scotch, if you have it. Neat if it's good stuff."

She poured from a bottle into two tumblers and then stepped out from behind the bar, handing one to Slater and sinking into a puffy chair. Slater sat across the coffee table from her, on the sofa, and tipped his glass toward her, then took a tentative sip. It was nutty, and woody, and perfect.

"You like the scotch?" she asked, watching him.

"It's absolutely delicious."

She smiled, clearly pleased. "I found it when I was over there. At a distillery. You can't even buy it here—they keep the best stuff for themselves."

"You're a connoisseur."

"Not really."

"Do you work?" Slater said, swirling his tumbler and taking another sip.

"I don't have to. Abner has adequate resources."

"I see that. This is a great house." He gestured to the room. "It strikes me as a lot of house for an accountant running his own shop. His office in K-town looks like it's just him."

Marisol sat forward. "You went to Abner's office?"

"This morning."

"What did he say?"

"He's not happy that you hired me. I think I pissed him off. He was shouting by the time I left."

"Good," she said emphatically, and raised her glass toward him.

"Does he have family money?"

"Abner always said he was a self-made man."

"Last night you implied that he was hiding assets from you. Where is it all coming from?"

"I'm as much in the dark as you are," she said, holding his gaze. "I know he has investments. Ideally I'd like to find out about those."

"You hired me to tell him to back off," Slater said, "which I've done. I'm not an accountant."

"Of course." Marisol rose and went to the credenza at the side of the room, returning with a piece of folded notepaper. She handed it to him and sat down again, sipping at her scotch.

It was a handwritten street address with an apartment number.

"What's this?" Slater said.

"It's connected to Abner."

"What's at this address?"

"I have no idea."

Slater frowned. "Where did you get it?"

"Abner took my car last week. That was in the GPS."

"Was it the only place he went?"

"He drove to his office, and some businesses where his clients are, and the drugstore—all explainable, except for that one," she said, unabashed to admit to invading Abner's privacy. "I wrote it down because I couldn't identify it. I checked online. It looks like an apartment building."

Slater studied the note, in her looping handwriting, and took a gulp of the heady scotch. He'd never seen GPS navigation that used an apartment number, so she was lying about where this had come from.

"Shouldn't your lawyer be looking into this?" Slater said. "It's different than just being afraid of him."

"I need all the information I can get to keep myself safe," she said, her eyes growing wide.

"Bullshit," Slater said flatly. "What's really going on?"

Her expression shifted, dropping the feigned innocence. "Lawyers don't have your skills. I suspect Abner is hiding things from me. You're better positioned to do that kind of research than some puffed-up deskbound ambulance-chaser."

That rang true, Slater decided, even though parts of it were still lies, including the shrinking-violet story she'd spun to him last night. Still, she was paying him.

"I'll see what I can do," he said, draining his tumbler and standing up.

"Do you need more money from me?" she asked, rising with him.

"I will, but not yet."

"Do you have to rush off?" she said, her eyes softening. "You liked the scotch—stay and have another. The night view of the city from the master is breathtaking."

"It's never going to happen, sister," he said flatly.

"Are you married or something? I didn't see a ring."

"I only date guys."

She sighed. "I should have seen that. I guess it's true that all the good ones are gay."

Slater raised his eyebrows. "I'm not a good one," he said, and walked out.

Marisol followed him to the front door to close it behind him as he left. The street was poorly lit, like the streets always were in the hills, as he went back to his car. Checking into the address she'd given him could wait for tomorrow, he decided, climbing in and navigating back toward civilization.

Turning onto Hyperion, his phone, sitting on the passenger seat, sounded with an idiosyncratic ringtone: *"No wire hangers … ever! I buy you three-hundred-dollar dresses, and you treat them like they were some dishrag!"* Swiping at it to answer, he pressed the speaker button.

"What do you need, Doris?" he demanded.

"Am I not allowed to say hello to my son?" she said.

"Conrad said you've been gossiping about my private stuff. You need to stop talking to him."

"That's not your call, sweetie. He was curious about your romantic life."

"I'm not romancing anyone," Slater said, his voice rising, glancing in his side mirror and gunning the engine to merge onto the 5.

"Of course not. Listen, do you have some time this week? My bougainvillea is getting pretty wild."

Slater sighed. "I'll try to make time."

"I'll do a pizza for you with that fake cheese."

"Vegan food isn't fake. It's just vegan."

"You know what I mean," she said.

"Maybe tomorrow," he said, and ended the call.

Such a frustrating woman. Slater wanted her to move up the coast somewhere, like a normal retiree. San Luis Obispo was the place he'd picked, far enough from LA that she'd be out of his hair, and far enough from the Bay Area that the real estate hadn't become insanely overvalued.

Back in his own alley, he eased into his garage and killed the engine, waiting for the door to roll down. Trotting up the stairs, he eyed the bourbon bottle on the counter as he went in. That stuff wasn't nearly as satisfying as Marisol's scotch, but it was definitely cheaper. Not yet, though. Guys first, then booze.

Once he'd stretched out in his recliner, he opened the hookup app on his phone. It was a little early to get the widest variety, but maybe more of the guys would be sober. Scrolling through the torsos, faces, and other body parts, he got a message from someone who'd seen him come online:

U hawt. Smack me around?

The guy looked ordinary, showing the stockiness of middle age, and in his face pic he was making duck lips. That alone merited smacking around. Overall he seemed nerdy, and probably sane, and had peroxide-blond hair. Slater sent him a reply:

My place. No drugs.

Adding his address, he scanned through other options until he got a reply:

Be there in 10.

Slater tucked his phone away and rose, picking up the laundry from the bedroom floor and dumping it in the closet, hiding the booze, and then changing into a tight white T-shirt. Guys always loved that look, for some reason, denim and a white T-shirt, like a blank canvas to project their desires onto.

When the knock came at the door, he twisted the deadbolt and pulled it open. The guy was older than in his photos, but not egregiously so. He was wearing baggy cargo shorts and a red polyester golf shirt that showed his nipples.

"You look like your profile pic," the guy said, grinning at him.

"I know. I was there when I took it."

Stepping inside, he looked around. "Whoa—

what a dump." Turning to Slater, he added, "And I'm not doing Bette Davis."

Slater folded his arms. "I'm glad we cleared that up. What's your name?"

"Dave," he said, and stepped closer. "Damn, you're hot."

"So what did you mean by 'smack me around'?"

"I like it a little rough, but I don't want bruises."

"So you want me to slap you, but not punch you."

"I guess."

"Don't guess," Slater said sharply. "Tell me what you want. What's your ideal sex thing?"

"With you," Dave said, eyeing him, "maybe you'd overpower me, slap me around a little, no bruises—"

"You said that part."

"Right. Then tie me up. You'd do it with your clothes on." He stepped closer, and put his hands on Slater's biceps, avoiding his gaze and giving them a gentle squeeze.

"I can do that," Slater said. "I have some rope in the garage. I'll be right back."

As he moved toward the door, Dave said, "You're very trusting."

"I've got something you want," Slater said, "so I know you'll behave. Besides, there's nothing to steal."

Dave scowled at him. "Right, like that's the

first thing I thought of when I stepped in here: *I'm going to jack this guy.*"

Slater chuckled as he went out, trotting down the stairs and unlocking his garage. From the wall rack with his gardening stuff he took a folding knife and a coil of rope. It was thin-gauge hemp, meant for yard work, holding saplings to their support posts and training wisteria, but doubled up, it wouldn't leave any marks on the blond.

Stepping into the hallway again, at the top of the stairs, he found a diminutive woman with a cloud of gray hair, standing in front of the door adjacent to his, twisting her keys in the lock. Wearing a baggy cardigan and a plaid skirt, she looked up at him with watery eyes.

"How are you, Grace?" Slater said.

"I'm glad I ran into you, dear. If you have a minute, one of my smoke detectors is blipping."

"Can I drop by later this week? I kind of have a date right now."

Grace looked pointedly at the coil of rope, then grinned at him. "I wouldn't want to keep you from that."

"Thanks. Do you have fresh batteries?"

"All I need is someone to climb on a chair and swap it out. Anyway, have fun."

Back in his apartment, he closed the door and flipped the deadbolt. Dave was standing at the end of the living room, gazing out the grimy window at the street below. He turned to Slater as he walked in.

"What the hell do you think you're doing?" Slater demanded.

Dave frowned. "Looking at the laundry place across the street."

Slater threw the rope to the carpet, his lip twisting into a sneer. "I step away for one minute, and you pull this."

Alarm flickered in Dave's eyes, but then he figured out what was happening.

"I don't want any trouble," he said, holding up his palms.

"Too late." Slater stepped over to him and slapped him hard, left and then right, a rapid kovac. Dave gasped and dropped his chin, holding his gaze as his face went red. Grabbing a wrist, Slater spun the guy around, effortlessly because he wasn't resisting it, and shoved his arm up his back. Pressing him against the wall, Slater growled in his ear, "You messed with the wrong man."

Dave exhaled, closing his eyes, exhilarated. Slater kneed him in the back of the leg, and Dave collapsed onto the filthy carpet. Slater straddled him, pulling off his golf shirt, then unbuckled his belt and pulled off his shorts. The guy was already hard. Grabbing the rope, Slater deftly tied his wrists together behind his back, using a simple stop knot, then cut the rope short with the knife and rolled Dave onto his side, squeezing his cock.

"Yeah, man," Dave said, breathing hard. "This is so freaking hot."

Slater slapped him and said, "Shut up."

Unfazed, Dave said breathily, "Do you want to hogtie me? Just not on my neck. I can't go to work with rope burn."

"You think I'm a dilettante?" Slater said, and slapped him again.

He tied Dave's feet together, then looped the rope between that bond and the one at his wrists, leaving it loose enough that he could move around. Dave struggled for a minute, ecstatic, and Slater sat back, watching him.

"Come on, man," Dave said finally. "Make me come. Do it."

Slater grabbed the knife and cut a length of rope, doubling it and then knotting it in the middle. Stuffing the knot in his mouth, he tied the rope behind Dave's head. Not having much say in the matter, Dave's eyes grew wide. Slater grabbed his cock, pumping it gently at first, kissing him around the rope gag. As Slater worked him, Dave came, grunting and heaving and panting, then slumped to the carpet.

Once he was still, Slater took up the knife and cut the rope gag, then moved to cut the other bonds.

"Not yet," Dave said, and ran his tongue on

the side of his mouth, reddened by the rope. "Come on, I'll blow you."

Slater unbuttoned his jeans and pulled out his cock, already hard.

"You're cut," Dave said. "Latin guys aren't usually cut."

"I'm Jewish, and Jewish guys are always cut."

Dave's eyes narrowed. "You're Jewish?"

"Man, shut up," Slater said, and shoved his cock in Dave's mouth, careful not to gag him in his powerless prone position. Dave had done this before, showing dexterity and skill, and before long, Slater came, groaning and then pulling away.

After he caught his breath, he cut Dave loose, rubbing his wrists once they were free of the rope. Dave sprawled on his back, recovering, and Slater ran a hand through his hair.

"How often do you have to put the color in?" Slater asked.

"I don't—this is natural."

"OK," Slater said, eyeing the dark roots and furrowing his brow.

"That was amazing," Dave said. "You have all the gear."

"It's just gardening stuff."

"Still, you know what you're doing."

Slater shrugged. "I kind of do it for a living."

"Tying people up?"

"Manhandling lowlifes."

"That sounds unsavory," Dave said.

"I suppose it is, but I get paid."

"Why do you have gardening tools? There isn't a speck of green in this neighborhood."

"I used to do that for a living."

"You're kind of odd," Dave said, watching him. "Did anyone ever tell you that?"

"Continually."

"Can I get your number?"

"Look for me in the app," Slater said, standing up.

As Dave got dressed, Slater noticed he had a bit of rope burn on one cheek, at the side of his mouth, where the gag had been. No way was he going to say anything about it. Hopefully it would fade in a day or so.

After the guy left, Slater went into the bedroom and swapped his jeans for a pair of boxer shorts, then to the kitchen to get the bourbon from the cupboard. Eyeing the bottle, he hoped there was enough. He couldn't very well go out half lit to get more, and he wasn't willing to pay to get it delivered. Guzzling from the bottle and coughing at the burn, he poured a tumbler full and killed the lights, stretching out on the sofa.

The music on the radio wasn't good yet, as it wasn't late enough, so he put on *Sasquatch Search,* a podcast he listened to sometimes. The narrator's tone was calm and methodical, even when dramatic things happened, like finding a strand of hair on the branch of a tree, or stumbling across an oversize footprint in the soft bank of a stream, or hearing a guttural wail from beyond the next ridge. Mostly the story was about the journey, the calm quest for the legendary cryptid deep in the woods. Slater sank into the words as the amber warmth suffused from his belly and pulled him downward into unconsciousness.

———◆———

Waking in bed, he tried to remember climbing in, but his memory was vague. At least his head didn't hurt. Getting up, he stepped over the shirt and shorts he'd been wearing, strewn on the floor, and went to look at his face in the bathroom mirror, then washed and took the time to shave. He was seeing Doris today, so he had to, although he wasn't sure why—she'd never say anything about him looking scruffy, as she wasn't a stereotypical Jewish mother with the guilt trips. Maybe he wanted her to think he was civilized enough to run a razor over his face once in a while.

In the kitchen he fished a pickle out of the jar, then ate some olives, standing over the trash to spit out the pits. After he got dressed, he grabbed a clean shirt, carrying it on its hanger. On the way out he found an empty bourbon bottle in front of the door. Stooping, he snatched it up and set it on the counter. He must have put it there to remind himself to buy more.

In the garage he hung the shirt in the back-seat of the Thunderbird, then pulled his hedge trimmer from the wall rack and loaded it into the trunk, and took his pair of heavy gauntlets, to deal with the spiky bougainvillea. As he climbed into the car, he fished in his pocket for the slip of paper Marisol had given him, then punched the address into the map on his phone. It was in North Hollywood, out in the Valley. Slater backed out of the garage, navigating toward the 101.

As Marisol had said, the address was an apartment building, on a busy street and half a block long. It was the kind they built in the 1950s, four floors of apartments around a central courtyard, and he'd bet money there was a pool in the middle. After he parked down the block, he walked back to find the entry door locked. A woman with leathery tanned skin and bottle-blond straw-dry hair was standing inside the glass, digging paper out of one of the mailboxes. Noticing him try the door, she pushed open the latch for him.

"Are you here to fix the pool?" she said. "The water's freezing. You need to crank up the heat."

"I'm not the help," Slater snapped, and went to the stairwell, trotting up two flights and then walking along the hallway, open on one side to the courtyard below. Checking the slip of paper

Marisol had given him, he found the door marked 311 and rang the bell.

A woman opened the inner door, peering out at him from behind the screen. Slender, with dark hair like Marisol, and the same big eyes, she was significantly younger, and based on the way she was dressed, in sweatpants and a stretchy top, she hailed from a lower economic stratum than Marisol.

"I'm looking for Abner," Slater said.

She frowned. "Who are you?"

"A friend. Is he coming tonight?"

"Who wants to know?" she said sharply.

Slater put his hands on his hips. "You know, things were just fine when Abner was on his knees sucking my dick, but then I got wind he had a side piece over here."

The woman threw open the screen door and came at Slater, pounding his chest with the sides of her fists.

"I'm no side piece, you freak," she screamed. "You're the side piece."

She landed a few blows before Slater managed to shove her away, which took little effort, as she was half his size.

But she came at him again, shouting, "You— you're the side piece."

Slater slapped her, on one side and then the other, a solid kovac, then grabbed her upper arms and gave her a shake. "Settle down. You can't just assault people who knock on your door."

Red-faced, she took a step back. "I can't believe he's sleeping with you."

Slater studied her face, saw the hurt in her eyes. "Yeah, I might have made that part up. But obviously you're sleeping with him."

"Why did you come here? Did he send you?" She jabbed a finger at him. "You tell him he needs to man up."

"Save your anger for Abner."

"Abner's an asshole," she said, and folded her arms.

"So dump him," Slater said, throwing up his hands.

Her eyes grew wide. "Why would I ever do that? Why would you say that?" Looking him up and down, she added, "Are you really sleeping with him?"

Slater scoffed, and turned to leave.

"Fuck you, and fuck Abner," she shouted after him, her voice echoing in the courtyard. After a moment, she added, "I'm calling the cops."

Slater sighed. It didn't matter if she called them or not. He hadn't done anything actionable, and he'd be miles from here by the time they showed up. If they showed up.

Man up, she'd said. That implied Abner either wasn't coming around often enough, or not paying for enough stuff. Back on the street, Slater walked toward his car, glancing over his shoulder to make sure she hadn't tailed him. She was definitely a girlfriend, with all that anger toward the guy. Abner clearly had a type. But it seemed unlikely he was going to trade in the Mustang for the Fiesta. No, he was definitely stringing this woman along.

FOUR

The map told him to take the 5, and half an hour later he was in Mount Washington, pulling into Doris's driveway. Her Buick was here, but thankfully there was no sign of her dumb-ass boyfriend's stupid midlife-crisis Boxster. Pulling up behind the Buick, he opened his trunk and put on the gauntlets, then carried the hedge trimmer through the gate at the side of the house into the backyard.

Doris was right—her hedge needed work. Long canes of bougainvillea shot out from the top at all angles, gently bobbing in the breeze. The roses on the other side needed work too, but it was better to leave those until January. Firing up the hedge trimmer, he walked the length of the yard, the sheared branches tumbling around him. Ideally the top of the hedge would be a little higher, but climbing on a ladder was too much work, so he topped it as high as he could reach.

After one last pass, he found the rake and Doris's green bin, and soon had everything cleaned up, the bin at the curb, the gloves and the hedge trimmer back in his trunk.

Doris greeted him at the front door. Petite, with her dark hair going gray, today she was wearing a black sweater and jeans. Slater stooped to kiss her hello.

"You look sweaty," she said. "Maybe hot food was the wrong choice."

"It'll be fine," he said, and went to wash up.

On the table in the dining room he found the promised pizza, topped with thin tomato slices and basil leaves, along with two plates and a pitcher of water.

"Where's your boyfriend?" Slater said, pulling out a chair.

"Probably working. I don't see him every day."

"Good," he said emphatically, and pulled a slice of pizza onto his plate.

Doris wasn't an accomplished cook, but she did a few things well, and this was one of them, a reasonable reward for doing her yard work.

"The hedge looks great now," she said, setting aside an uneaten crust. "So lovely and uniform."

"You have to keep on top of it," Slater said.

"It's been warm this year. The basil plant is still producing."

"I see that," Slater said, taking a bite with a wilted basil leaf.

"I put it on right at the end, so it cooked just a little."

"It's delicious," he said, and took another slice, enjoying the flavors and the crispy crust.

"So I was reading about AA," Doris said, once he'd finished eating.

"Good god, woman," he spluttered, slamming down his water glass.

"Slater—count," she said sharply.

He pressed his lips together and glared at her. It was a tactic she had used on him when he was a kid, theoretically to make him focus, but really it was just to shut him up so that she could talk over him. It was pretty damn nervy of her to do that to him as a grown man.

"I'm not telling you what to do," she said, her tone calmer. "I just want you to think about a couple of things."

Slater folded his arms and waited.

Pulling out her phone, she tapped at it. "You don't have to answer these. Just think about it." Reading from the screen, she said, "Do you prefer to drink alone?"

Of course he drank alone—why would he

drink with other people? The question made no sense.

"Do you ever have memory loss because of drinking?"

"That's kind of the point," he said.

Doris frowned and looked back at her screen. "Do you avoid being honest about your drinking?"

"I wish I could. Then you and Conrad wouldn't be all up in my grill about it."

"What about Andy? Has he weighed in?"

"He knows better than to try."

"All I ask is that you think about your life, and your health."

"Stop worrying about me," Slater said irritably.

"I'm your mother. That's basically my job description."

"I'm not thirteen anymore."

Doris threw up her hands. "He speaks the truth. So do you want another slice?"

"I should get back to work."

"You don't need to shower?"

"I brought a clean shirt," he said, and got up.

Doris walked him to the door. "Are you around on Saturday? I'm going to a protest downtown with some of the girls."

"I have to work. But have fun." Stooping to kiss her, he added, "Love you."

She squeezed his arm, and stood inside the screen door as he went to the driveway, pulling his clean shirt out of the car and changing into it.

Doris had closed the door by the time he got behind the wheel, tossing his sweaty shirt in the backseat. He dialed Marisol's number.

"Can I see you today?" he said, when she picked up.

"I'm on the way to my club. You can ask for me at the desk," she said, and rattled off an address, ending with "South Pasadena."

Slater didn't really know that part of town, but it wasn't far from Doris's neighborhood, and he backed out of the driveway, navigating toward the 110. On the way he pulled into the lot of a strip-mall liquor store and went inside. They kept the good stuff behind the counter, and Slater pointed it out.

"Three fifths of the black label," he told the clerk.

As she took them down, the woman asked, "Having a party?"

Slater frowned, ignoring the question, and pulled out his wad of cash, setting the bills on the counter. "Wrap each of them separately before you put them in the bag."

On the way out, his phone buzzed in his pocket, and he pulled it out to check as he climbed into his car. Andy had sent a text:

Got some info for you.

Navigating off the freeway in South Pas, Slater soon found the address of Marisol's club, a long, low midcentury building with big blocky eaves. Back in its original incarnation it might have been offices, or a warehouse, or even a bowling alley, but today the sign out front bore hot pink lettering that read CHEZ YELENA. Nosing into the arcing driveway, he stopped at the valet desk, where a chubby mustachioed guy in a maroon vest held the car door when he opened it.

The guy said something in Spanish, and Slater shrugged and said, "Sorry."

"Nice wheels," he said cheerfully, his English flawless. "What year is it?"

"It's a '78."

Slater stepped toward the building as the guy climbed in and pulled away. The place had stupid lush grass landscaping, like a putting green. They must not have heard how irresponsible that was. A Persian silk tree on the lawn stood too close to the building, but that mistake had been made decades ago. Right now it needed to be limbed up.

As he neared the entrance, a thick-set guy, shiny skin showing through his thinning hair on top, stepped out, subtly giving him the once over. African hair looked better cut short when you started losing it, but this guy seemed unconcerned. He was wearing a suit with a gold name tag that said MICHAEL.

"You look like management," Slater said.

"What can I do for you?" he said affably.

"Tell your gardener the silk tree needs to be pruned," Slater said, pointing it out.

"It's actually a mimosa tree."

"That's one of the names people use," Slater said. "It's not what I call it. I suppose that's why we use Latin names, so that we can all agree on what the hell we're talking about."

Michael grinned. "You know the Latin name of our tree?"

"Genus *Albizia*," Slater said flatly, holding his gaze. "I'd have to look up the other part. It's an invasive, but that's no reason to neglect it. Get it pruned."

Stepping around him into the lobby, Slater found a long counter staffed by three women, all in white blouses, with the same gold name tag that Michael wore. The space was sleek, with lots of white surfaces and blond wooden furniture. If the point was to make the place look upscale, it worked, and having three clerks dressed like medical technicians perched on stools and doing nothing projected extravagance even more effectively than the contemporary decor.

Slater stopped in front of one of them, in her twenties, with heavy eye makeup, her black hair in an updo. Her gold tag read YUMIKO.

"I have a meeting with Marisol Hart," Slater told her.

"One moment," she said, and picked up a phone, murmuring into it, "Is Marisol available?" She listened for a moment, then replaced the receiver and met Slater's gaze. "She's in a treatment room, but she said to bring you in anyway. Follow me."

Yumiko slid off her stool and walked to a side door, pushing out into a courtyard. Patio tables and chaises longues were positioned around under shade trees. It would be nice here in spring, Slater thought, following her, but right now it was too cold for lounging, and no one was using the space. The trees looked like jacarandas, and these, at least, were properly limbed up. Michael needed to get this gardener working out front.

"What is this place?" Slater said, catching up to his guide.

"We call it a club, and it is membership-driven, but it's more of a day spa," Yumiko said, glancing at him. "Massages, skin treatments, even some classes."

"Mostly women?"

She smiled. "Seventy percent. We get lots of couples."

Stepping through a doorway into another building, she led him down a hallway and opened a door, tacitly holding it for Slater and then closing it as he stepped inside.

The room was dimly lit, and in the middle of the floor stood a medical-grade recliner, its occupant wearing a white bathrobe, hair in a towel, and a mask over her face, glowing an eerie red at the edges. Wires ran from the mask to an electronic box, mounted on a rolling stand, with a number readout and a set of controls. The gear wouldn't look out of place in a hospital room. At one side, in an ordinary chair, sat a buxom woman dressed in the same white uniform as Yumiko, her hair in a tight Afro with a blue band in it. She looked up from her phone as he came in.

"Marisol?" Slater said, peering at the eye holes in the mask.

"I'm sorry I can't sit up."

It really was Marisol—her voice and lilting accent were unmistakable.

"I'm under the lamps for another half hour," she said, and waved a hand. "Cathy, could you give us a minute?"

"Of course," the woman said, and rose. "Buzz if you need me."

When she'd gone and they were alone, Marisol gestured vaguely. "Sit down."

Slater shifted the chair closer so that he could at least see her eyes.

"What's the mask for?" he asked.

"It reverses aging of the collagen molecules."

"That sounds like a miracle."

"You sound like a skeptic."

"Maybe," Slater said. "Just don't tell me how much it costs."

"You implied that you had news."

He leaned toward her. "Where did you really get that address in NoHo?"

"I told you—Abner drove there. I found it in the GPS. Why don't you believe that?"

"It's an apartment," Slater said, "occupied by a woman."

"A mistress," Marisol said, and was quiet for a moment.

The only sign of her reaction to the information was rapid blinking. It wasn't enough to tell whether she was feeling anger, or hurt, or something else.

"I guess I'm not surprised," Marisol said finally. "What does she look like?"

"Latin, wiry, maybe thirty."

"Is she prettier than me?"

He gazed at the weird glowing mask, the gaps for her mouth and eyes, the white hair wrap, making her look like a science-fiction villain. "Not even close. Is it information that will help you in the divorce?"

"I hope so." She eyed him. "Do you know for sure that she's sleeping with Abner?"

"I asked," Slater said, watching her. "Indirectly,

but she confirmed it."

Marisol looked away.

"I have some other feelers out. I'm not sure if I'll learn anything significant. If not, what you've paid me covers the work I've done."

"I can pay you more if you uncover more. You seem to be good at this."

"I'll let you know," Slater said, and rose.

"Wait," she said. "Can you do one more thing? Tell him I know about the woman in NoHo."

Slater frowned. "Tell him yourself. Or have your lawyer do it."

"It's better coming from you," she said. "More intimidating. You're still working for me, aren't you?"

"Sure. I can talk to Abner."

"You should go armed."

Slater met her gaze. "Why? Does he have a weapon?"

"When he moved out, he started carrying a gun. You need to protect yourself. Abner is vicious—who knows what he's capable of."

"I'll keep that in mind," he said, and closed the door behind him, walking toward the front building and the lobby.

No way was he going to skulk around with a heater. That's how people got shot. Was Abner really that guy? It wasn't easy to start carrying a concealed weapon based on a whim. Not here, not legally, anyway. No, it felt more like maybe Marisol wanted him to show up at Abner's with a gun. He'd be wary of Abner, of course, but more significantly, he needed to figure out what Marisol was up to.

Waiting for the valet to retrieve his car, he checked his phone and found a text from Conrad:

Call me.

It was irksome, being told what to do by that stupid ape, but he might have useful information. He dialed Conrad's number.

"I'm going off shift soon," Conrad said when he answered. "Do you want to grab a bite at that place on Sunset with the crazy menu?"

"Do you have something for me?" Slater demanded.

"I was going to tell you all that when we met."

"Fine," he said flatly, "but you're buying."

"I'm doing you a favor," Conrad said, "which means you're buying."

Slater sighed audibly. "I'm in South Pas right now. I'm on my way."

Pocketing his phone, Slater palmed a fin and stepped around to meet the valet, who left the motor running as he climbed out of the Thunderbird.

"How much?" Slater asked him.

"It's complementary, sir."

Slater slipped him the fin before climbing in, then pulled out of the driveway, navigating back to the 110.

Cruising along Sunset, he found a street space a block before the diner and pulled in, pausing on the sidewalk to feed the meter. It was way too early for dinner, and when he walked into the leafy courtyard, only a few tables were occupied. Conrad sat alone at one, next to a gas heater, wearing a blue plaid shirt and reading the menu. Looking up as Slater approached, he flashed that beautiful smile.

"What?" Slater demanded, pulling out the chair across from him.

"It's nice to see you," Conrad said. "Jesus, Slater, chill out."

"What's with the shirt?"

Conrad ignored that. "Doris said you trimmed her bougainvillea."

"I just did that. How often do you two talk?"

"I'm glad you're taking care of her."

"That's really none of your damn business," Slater said, his eyes narrowing, "and I'll warn you now, if you say one word about twelve-step, I'm going to punch you in the face."

The waiter stopped beside the table, his brow furrowed in concern. "Before you get to the fisti-cuffs, would you like to order?"

"The burger with the slaw," Conrad said.

"You do a curry thing with garbanzos," Slater said, eyeing him.

The waiter nodded. "It comes with jasmine rice or buttermilk biscuits."

"Rice," Slater said.

Once he'd left, Conrad said, "It's not a great idea to punch a cop."

"You're off duty."

"Even so, think about it. I ask you to eat out, a pleasant meal in a cozy spot, and the first thing you do is threaten me with violence."

Slater took a deep breath, stifling his initial reaction. "I'd never do anything to mar that perfect face."

Conrad nodded, suppressing a grin. "Thank you," he said, and sipped at his water. "So I checked on your feuding couple. Which one is your client?"

"The woman."

"There's no record on her before she got her green card, six years ago. She's from Argentina."

"That checks out with what she told me," Slater said.

"I can't get records from the old country, but here she's kept her nose clean."

"What about Abner?"

"He's never been popped, but he's been in court a lot," Conrad said. "Sued three times in civil court over bankruptcies and debts."

"The guy's an accountant. In his world, maybe that makes sense."

"Still, it seems like a lot. All that stuff happened a while ago. In recent years he seems to have kept out of trouble."

The food arrived, and they tucked in, and Slater managed to be civil, asking Conrad about his work. Conrad told him a wild story about a colleague who'd helped deliver a baby on the side of the freeway. He waved his fork for emphasis as he talked, his eyes bright. Slater watched, munching on his curry. Just looking at Conrad, seeing his animated expressions, listening to his voice, Slater felt an ache in the pit of his stomach.

After Slater had paid the waiter, they stood up.

"Thanks for your help," Slater said.

Conrad's eyebrows shot up. "Any time," he said. "Take care of yourself."

They walked out to the street together, the end of the day glowing orange in the western sky.

"I'm back this way," Slater said.

Conrad gave him a brief bro hug and walked off in the other direction.

The guy wasn't a total jerk, Slater thought, walking back to his car. He could be civil sometimes. Seeing him this evening felt like when they'd been together, the part when things had been good, when they'd agreed on everything, fit each other, laughed all the time. But focusing on that just magnified the loss, the inevitable knowledge that they would never be together again. It was easier to remember the part with all the shouting, and acrimony, and shattered crockery, and getting kicked to the curb.

Climbing into the Thunderbird, he phoned Andy.

"You've got something for me?" Slater said when he picked up.

"My big dick," Andy said.

Slater chuckled. "Can I come over?"

"You know where I'm at."

The drive downtown took a while in the traffic, but eventually Slater pulled into the lot next to Andy's building and went upstairs. When Andy came to the door, he looked sleepy, wearing a T-shirt and boxers. Slater embraced him once they were inside, kissing his mouth, then his shaggy cheek, and his neck.

"So where's this big dick I've heard so much about?" Slater said.

Andy pulled back and met his gaze. "I'm not sure you can … handle it."

"That sounds like a challenge."

Sitting on the end of the bed, Andy steadied himself by leaning back on his arms. "I'm going to fuck you senseless," he said. "Keep your hands where … I can see them, and take off your clothes. Nice and slow."

Slater couldn't help but grin. "This is something new. Demanding Andy."

"I thought I'd try it out," he said. "Is it working?"

Slater squeezed his crotch, his cock swelling in his jeans. "Signs point to yes."

Andy beamed, then went back into character. "What did I just … say?"

Slater held up his palms, then unbuttoned his shirt, methodically, gazing at Andy. Next he unbuckled his belt and dropped his jeans. Once he was completely naked, he knelt in front of Andy and pulled off his T-shirt, then slid off his boxers, revealing his raging hard-on. Shifting them both up the bed, Slater grabbed a condom from the bedside table. He rolled it onto Andy and squeezed his cock, eliciting a gasp, then climbed up and slid onto him, wincing with the intensity of it.

Leaning in to kiss him, Andy started thrusting, gently at first. With his mouth on Slater's, he built up to bucking wildly, fists flailing against Slater's thighs, and then he came, his face contorted. With Andy still inside him, Slater stroked himself, groaning as he climaxed, then collapsed beside him, sweaty and sticky and contented.

Later, when Andy stirred, Slater woke to find his arm around his chest, his belly in the small of his back, their bodies folded together.

Andy pulled away and shifted to face him. "So I looked into your accountant."

"Abner," Slater said.

"Right. I worked up a client list, or at least a partial version."

"Where did you find that?"

"I didn't really find it. I worked back from … other data. I collated everyone who mentions him or cites him in legal proceedings. A lot of his clients are kind of shady."

"Like who?" Slater said.

"I'll email you the list. One of them might be

a gangster, if you believe the rumors, and there's a pot distributor. Lots of that business is still in the gray economy. And there's the Church of the Early Bright."

"Oh, yeah, I've heard of it. Those people are freaking crazy." Slater sighed. "So if he works for a bunch of lowlifes, it implies the guy is a lowlife himself."

"There's more," Andy said, raising an eyebrow. "The guy wears one of those fitness trackers, and he didn't put a very strong password on his account."

"I don't really need to know how many steps he takes every day."

"The one he wears has location tracking, so there's a record of everywhere he's been since he bought it."

Slater met his eye. "Seriously?"

"That's huge, right? I put it all in a spreadsheet, and I did some preliminary work cross-referencing the locations with his clients. It actually helped me figure out who some of them were."

"Right on," Slater said, running a hand through Andy's hair. "That'll help a lot."

"There's lots of spurious places, like restaurants. Dude eats out every single day. One that caught my eye was the Baltimore Hotel—he goes once a week or so, always in the evening, and only for a short time, like forty to seventy minutes."

"Too brief for a hookup."

"Enough time for a meal, but he usually hits an eatery earlier."

"He's going to the bar," Slater said. "I know that place. It's suitably glam for a fancy guy like Abner."

"A drink or two," Andy said. "That fits the time frame. A more interesting destination, though, is Albuquerque."

"When was he there?"

"He goes once a month, just for the day. Flies out in the morning, back in LA by evening. From the airport he always goes to the same address and spends a couple hours. He doesn't make any other stops, not even a taco stand."

"OK, that sounds suspicious."

"From what I can see online, the location is a standalone bar. I thought it might be another shady client, so I checked on the ownership. It's held by a company called High-Level Prestige Co. That part seems odd, because in the street view the place is small and ordinary, almost like a dive bar. There's nothing prestigious about it."

"It's him," Slater said, sitting up on his elbows. "That's exactly the kind of language he uses on his website. Abner has to be High-Level Prestige Co."

"You'll probably see more in the location data

than I did. I just cherry-picked the fun stuff, like the Baltimore and a repeating day trip to Albuquerque."

"Damn, you're good," Slater said, eyeing him appreciatively.

Andy grinned. "I'm going to have to bill you for about six hours."

"It's worth every dime, brother, and more. So with the fitness tracker, can you see where Abner is in real time?"

"Probably," Andy said. "The device uploads data every few minutes when it's in range of his cell phone, which is presumably always."

"Can you give me the login?"

"Sure—grab your phone."

Slater rolled to the side of the bed and found his jeans, pulling out his phone and then turning back.

Andy told him the website to pull up, then recited Abner's user name and password.

"How do you have that stored in your brain?" Slater demanded, glancing at him as he thumb-typed. "It's a stupid password, but still."

He chuckled. "I have a good memory."

Once he was into Abner's account, Slater tapped through the contents until he found the location history. It was set up to show his activity as trips in list form and on a map, where a tangle of blue lines connected the end points.

The most recent segments today were a trip from the Durham Building to a hotel in Koreatown—Marisol had said he was living at a place like that—and then a trip from there to the Baltimore. Clicking on the end point, it was time-stamped just a few minutes ago.

"He's at the Baltimore now," Slater said, sitting up. "That's two blocks from here. What are the odds?"

"You want to go confront him?"

"I can do that at his office. I want to surveille him." He got up and hurriedly pulled on his jeans. "If he hangs out at a hotel bar, he's probably meeting someone. I want to know who."

"Come back afterward," Andy said. "You can stay over."

"I can't," Slater said, thinking of the three beautiful bottles in his trunk. As he buttoned his shirt, standing in the dim light at the end of the bed, he added, "But I like demanding Andy."

"Good. Maybe you'll be seeing more of him."

———·———

It was too good an opportunity to pass up, Abner hanging out in a bar a few minutes' walk away. Downstairs in the parking lot, he briefly opened the passenger door of the Thunderbird and grabbed the earpiece for his phone, along with his earbuds. If Abner really was meeting someone, maybe he could listen in.

On foot, Slater hustled over to the back entrance to the Baltimore. On the way he switched on his earpiece and pulled up the app that would turn it into a remote mike, allowing him to listen on his phone. The back entrance opened into an ornate barn-like tea room, deserted at this hour. Slater trotted up the curving staircase to the main lobby, slowing his pace as he approached the bar. The lighting was warm and low, and tables and lounge chairs were spread through several rooms, some of them separated by wooden screens for privacy.

He didn't have to hunt very long to find Abner. The guy was perched on a barstool, the back of his blond head and his scoliotic back unmistakable, his effete frame hunched over in his green suit. Sitting sideways, Abner was facing another man, older, wearing a dark jacket over an argyle sweater. His features put him in his sixties, at least, and even from across the room, in low light, Slater could tell that his anachronistic jet-black haircut was either a bad rug or a cheap dye job.

It was good luck that Abner had his back to most of the room. There was an empty barstool beside him, with a couple of women, dressed for the office in gray and tan, on the other side of it. Slater couldn't very well sit there and eavesdrop, but Abner was engaged in conversation, and maybe he wouldn't notice if he stopped there for a moment. There really was nothing to lose—even if he recognized Slater, this was a lively public place, and he could blow it off as a coincidence.

Striding toward the bar, trying to look nonchalant, he walked up to the empty stool and set his earpiece on it, toward the back, in the shadows. At the same time he reached across the bar and grabbed a menu card, nodding to the bartender as he plucked it and turned away.

Abner hadn't looked around, and his bewigged companion didn't glance at Slater either. They were both drinking scotch or bourbon, their wide glasses each containing a massive chunk of ice surrounded by amber liquid.

Retreating to the next room, Slater sat in an easy chair, on its own and partly behind a screen, just out of view of the bar. It should be close enough to maintain the link to his phone, he decided. And it was—when he plugged in his earbuds and tapped at the app, he could hear what was being said in the vicinity of the earpiece. It wasn't directional, so he could hear the woman on the other side of the empty stool, chatting to her friend, as clearly as Abner and the guy with the rug. Closing his eyes, he concentrated on pulling out the men's conversation.

"That's why using a private craft is so much safer," the older man was saying. "Every airport in the country has those dogs, but it's an easy boat ride to the Bahamas, and from there it's a short flight."

"And it's a domestic flight to Fort Lauderdale," Abner said. "I know they don't check those."

Slater started when someone touched his arm. With his eyes shut and his earbuds in, he hadn't noticed the waitress standing in front of him.

"Beer," Slater said quietly, pulling one of his earbuds out. "Whatever's on tap."

"Kronenbourg?" she offered.

"That works."

He shoved his earbud in again, focusing on the men's voices. But the women drowned them out with a fit of laughter, shrill and reverberating, and Slater had to turn down the volume. Once the hilarity had subsided, he could hear Abner speaking.

"I'm certain that I could help you move things more efficiently."

"We have runners who take care of that," the other man said. "We call them acolytes. They have it committed to muscle memory. So don't concern yourself with the shipments. Your role is on a higher level—you're doing the lord's work by helping us prepare them."

The lord's work. He was with the Church of the Early Bright, Slater realized. This was a business meeting. It fit—the bad rug definitely made the guy look like a religious nut, and Andy had identified the church as one of Abner's clients.

The waitress returned and set a pint glass of beer on the table beside him. Wordlessly, Slater dug out a twenty and handed it to her. Before he could focus on the voices again, the women on the adjacent stools broke into another fit of laughter, followed by a deafening *snap* that made Slater wince and yank out his earbuds. Leaning to look around the wooden screen toward the bar, he saw what had happened—one of them had shifted the empty stool, and his earpiece had fallen to the floor.

Reclining, he inserted his earbuds again, but there was only silence. The fall had either broken the device or switched it off. He tried to overhear Abner without the earbuds in, but it was impossible, with background music filling the space and so many conversations all around.

The waitress returned with his change, and before she left he gave her a single and stuffed the rest in his pants. Slater picked up the pint and took a drink. He couldn't very well go in and retrieve the earpiece; if he started hunting around on the floor and moving stools, Abner would definitely make him. It wouldn't be a serious loss not to get it back, and it might be broken anyway. Rising from the chair, he took another deep drink, preparing to leave. But glancing at the bar, he saw that Abner and his religious companion were on their feet too.

Dropping back into the chair, Slater gave them time to say their good-byes, straining to pick out their voices in the noisy room. There was a hearty laugh that might have been the religious nut, and then the businesswomen laughing again. A minute later, when he looked to the bar, Abner and the other guy were gone.

Glancing around as he walked toward the bar, they were nowhere in sight, and Slater pulled out the stool where he'd left his earpiece, squatting to scan the floor in the dim light.

"Did you lose a contact lens?" the woman sitting on the next stool asked, holding her hair back to look down at him.

"I left my earpiece here earlier," Slater said, and spotted it against the bar, scooping it up. "And here it is."

"Yay," the woman said. "Reunited, and it feels so good."

Slater grinned at that as he stood up again. These two had obviously been imbibing for a while.

Her companion on the next stool eyed Slater and said, "You should have a drink with us."

"You should," the other one said emphatically. "We'll celebrate the retrieval of lost electronics."

"I can't," he said, waggling the earpiece. "Calls

to make. Enjoy your evening."

Scanning the corridor as he left to make sure Abner wasn't still around, Slater headed out to the street, enjoying the cool evening air on the walk back to the Thunderbird. That had been informative. It sounded like the Church of the Early Bright was shipping something to the Caribbean that they didn't want Uncle Sam to know about. Inbound smuggling meant drugs, but outbound, it was usually cash. A sleazy church and its financial machinations were of no concern to him, but what was Abner's part in it? At the very least, the churchman trusted Abner enough to discuss the subterfuge frankly—and had implied that Abner was involved.

The drive to his apartment went fast in the light late-evening traffic. Heaving the bourbon bottles out of his trunk, he trudged up the stairs, stowing two of them in the kitchen cupboard. The third he twisted open, and the seal broke with a satisfying *crack*. Filling a tumbler, he slammed it, and then poured another, not bothering with the ice.

It was hitting him fast, and his head was swimming as he stretched out on the sofa, setting the tumbler on the carpet. Had he eaten today? Of course he had, with Doris, and with dick-smack Conrad. Sweet, beautiful, perfect Conrad. He took another slug, coughing at the burn in his throat, and then put his arm over his eyes, feeling the abyss encroaching. This was the best part of the day.

SIX

Slater started awake, feeling a pair of fingers on his neck and slapping them away. Fleeting panic made his heart pound as his eyes struggled to focus on a black shirt, with a name tag and a shiny badge on it. Conrad, he realized, looming over him, wearing his uniform, holding his phone to his ear.

"He's OK," Conrad said. "Yeah … I'll call you later." He dropped the phone into his pocket.

"What are you doing in my apartment?" Slater said, laboring to form the words, his tongue thick. It was hard to focus, and his head was throbbing.

"You called me last night," Conrad said, "or more accurately, early this morning. I was worried."

"How did you get in?"

"Doris gave me the key. She was worried too."

"I don't remember giving her a key," Slater said, and tried to sit up, quickly abandoning the effort and fighting a wave of nausea. "Why did you drag her into it?"

"You called her too, and she called me."

Slater rubbed his eyes, trying to remember, trying to think clearly with the roiling pain in his head. He couldn't remember calling anyone.

"It smells like the drunk tank in here," Conrad said. "I'm going to open a window."

"This one's painted shut. The one in the other room opens."

He stepped out, and Slater heard the window scraping in its frame. Returning a moment later, Conrad said, "Do you have a fan?"

"Why would I have a fan?" Slater said irritably.

Conrad sat on the side of the bed and held his gaze. "Slater, you have to dry out."

"Is that an order, officer?"

"Cut the crap," Conrad said, raising his voice. "This is insanity. You're killing yourself. I'm not going to let you do that to Doris."

Slater turned his head away. "What did I say to her?" he asked quietly.

"I don't know. It scared her."

"What did I say to you?"

"There's a time and a place for everything, and this is neither the time nor the place to talk about that." Conrad sighed. "Do you have any-thing to eat here?"

"I don't need food."

Conrad folded his arms and sat for a moment longer, watching him. "I have to go," he said finally. "Drink lots of water."

"Give me that key," Slater croaked, trying to sound authoritative.

"No way, brother," he said, and walked out. A moment later Slater heard the front door close, the deadbolt twist into place.

Again he tried to sit up, but it made him too nauseous, made his head spin. He closed his eyes, but that made it worse, so he stared at the ceiling and took slow, deep breaths.

Eventually he was able to sit up and put his feet on the floor. The cold draft from the open window felt good, and after a few minutes he was able to stand. In the bathroom he shook some ibuprofen into his mouth from the little bottle, then washed them down with a glass of water at the kitchen sink. It felt like it all might come up again, so he went back to bed, taking deep breaths, and fell asleep.

Later, when he woke up, he felt a little better. His phone was on the bedside table, and he scrabbled for it, working to focus on the clock. It was past noon. What a fucking waste of time.

Pushing himself out of bed and into the

bathroom, he looked at his face in the mirror. With bloodshot eyes, dark circles underneath, he looked like he'd been in a brawl. Staring at himself, he muttered, "Idiot."

In the kitchen he ate half a spoonful of peanut butter and found a little packet of saltines in the cupboard, eating them over the sink. It felt like they might come up, so he took deep breaths and walked over to look down at the street, the cool air from the open window brisk on his face. He waited a while to make sure his gut was stable, then went into the bedroom and got dressed.

Stepping out and locking his deadbolt, he knocked on Grace's door.

"You should check the peephole," he said when she pulled it open.

"I knew it was you." She stood aside for him to enter, her brow furrowing. "You look terrible."

"Rough night," he said, avoiding her gaze. "Which smoke detector?"

"In the bedroom. I'll get you a battery."

Grace went into the kitchen, and Slater glanced around her apartment. It was a mirror image of his own, the same size but cleaner, and with decent carpeting and real furniture, like bookshelves, a sofa, and a dining table next to the kitchen. The shelves were filled to capacity with books and framed photos, but the place wasn't cluttered.

Lifting a chair from beside the table, he carried

it into the bedroom and positioned it under the smoke detector. The bed was made, with a bright flowery duvet, and on the wall beside it hung an oil painting, portraying a low adobe building in the Southwestern desert.

Grace came in and handed him the battery, and Slater climbed on the chair, suddenly feeling lightheaded with the exertion. Reaching for the ceiling, he stabilized himself by bracing his fingers on the popcorn surface for a moment, taking deep breaths. Once he was confident he had his balance, he fiddled with the device, swapping out the battery, waiting a few seconds to make sure the indicator stayed green.

"That should do it," he said, climbing down, and carried the chair back to its place at the dining table.

"Thanks, sweetie," Grace said, following him to the front door. Concern clouded her expression as he stepped out. "Take care of yourself."

Trudging down the stairs to the garage, Slater breathed through his nose to combat the nausea. It was too warm in Grace's place. It felt better to sit, once he'd climbed into the Thunderbird, and he stayed there for a minute, breathing deeply, before he rolled up the garage door and headed for Koreatown.

Finding a street space near the Durham Building, Slater fed the meter and walked toward the entrance. A panel van was parked in the loading zone out front, the side marked WILLOW-BROOK FIBER in bright orange letters, and below it a lurid logo of a snakelike length of cable with red laser beams exploding from the tip. That guy he'd met in the hallway the other day must still be wiring the building.

When he went into the marbled lobby, the guard didn't even look up. During business hours it was just for show and to keep homeless people out, but after hours they probably checked everyone. He didn't need to be stealthy anyway, he reminded himself. This was just an errand for Marisol, acting as her avatar to figuratively spit in Abner's eye.

Pushing open the door to the receptionist's office, Slater found Abner there, along with the thick-built woman with the dark-rimmed glasses. Abner was standing over her desk, wearing a different green suit. It must be his signature color. Despite Abner's wussy demeanor, he had to admit the green looked good with the blond dye job. The way he was standing, leaning over with his right hand on his hip, Slater could see inside his jacket. The guy wasn't wearing a shoulder holster, and there were no telltale bulges around his hips either. Max was always strapped, so he knew it wasn't easy to conceal a handgun, even under a suit. Maybe Abner kept it in his desk, or maybe Marisol had been lying.

Looking up, Abner scowled at the sight of him. "What do you want?"

"A quick word," Slater said, and glanced at the receptionist.

Abner hesitated, his lip curling in disgust as he straightened up. But he said, "Come on back," and led the way into his office.

Abner stood behind his desk and folded his arms, framed by the bougie red horse painting. He must really value it, given its pride of place. Slater could see the fitness tracker, a gray band at Abner's wrist, like a watch with no face. Slater should probably be grateful—the guy had saved him a lot of work and expense by wearing that.

Waiting until the door had pulled itself closed, Abner said, "You look like you've been in a car accident."

"You look like a down-market accountant," Slater shot back.

"Why are you wasting my time?" he demanded.

"Marisol knows about the woman you have holed up in NoHo. She wanted to tell you it'll come up in the divorce negotiations."

Abner scoffed. "Like I care what she knows about that. What do you do for her, anyway? Are you more than just a goddamn keyhole peeper, spying on my private life?"

"You're one to talk," Slater said, and put his

hands on his hips. "I know you work for crooks, but I can't make up my mind about you, where you fit into it. Are you a full-on lowlife, or just on the fringes? Where does all your money come from?"

Leaning on his desk, Abner spoke intently. "You don't know who you're dealing with. If you mess with my business, I'll burn you to the ground."

Slater waved a palm. "There's nothing to burn. I don't have things like you do—this office, that obnoxious McMansion of a house, a wife and a girlfriend both."

"I can fix it so you'll never work in this town again."

"I don't work that much anyway," Slater said simply. "You know, you don't really have the swagger to pull off the whole intimidation thing."

"Fuck you," Abner spat.

"You're pretty high-strung, you know that? It must be real fireworks with that woman in NoHo. She's pretty high-strung too—she came at me. Do you ever wonder whether you should have stuck with Marisol?"

Abner stepped around the desk. "Get out," he shouted.

Slater raised his eyebrows, and thought fleetingly about asking what it was Abner wanted to help ship to the Bahamas, or mentioning the bar in Albuquerque. But he didn't need to show all his cards. As he turned to leave, Abner moved closer, and shoved his shoulder. Slater spun around and grabbed him by the lapels, slamming him against the wall. Abner slapped at his face, and Slater grabbed both his wrists, forcing them down, pressing his chest into Abner's, pinning him to the wall.

"You shouldn't have done that," Slater said.

Sweating and red-faced, Abner was breathing hard. "Come on. I wasn't trying to pick a fight."

Slater could smell his sour breath, feel his heart pounding. Against his thigh he felt a hard lump. Not releasing his grip on Abner's wrists, he shifted position.

"You've got wood," Slater said.

"You stupid fuck," Abner said, glaring at him, but then suddenly moved closer, kissing him.

Caught by surprise, Slater leaned into it, exploring his mouth. It had a weird taste, maybe tobacco or pot. Pressing his crotch into Abner's woody, he stayed with it a moment longer, then pulled away.

Abner went limp as Slater released his grip on his wrists, slouching against the wall, his head hanging, avoiding Slater's gaze.

"I wondered about you," Slater said, and turned to leave.

"Wait," Abner said, his tone plaintive.

Ignoring him, Slater pulled open the door

and walked past the receptionist. From the blank expression on her face as she glanced up, she hadn't overheard them.

No way was he going to sleep with the guy, he thought, riding down in the elevator. Abner was way too sleazy, and clearly not in touch with his gay side. More significant, why did he feel compelled to threaten Slater, who wasn't really a threat to him? It was a glaring overreaction. Maybe there was more to uncover.

Climbing into the Thunderbird, he sat for a minute with his eyes closed, breathing through his nose, willing the ache in his head to subside. Eventually he started the engine and pulled into the street, navigating to his office. The parking attendant waved as he climbed out and went across the street.

The lights were off, the office quiet. Glancing into Max's space, he went into his own, grabbing his keyboard and sitting with his feet on the desk. In the factories above and below he could he hear the faint sound of sewing machines cycling on and off.

Andy had emailed him Abner's client list, and he researched several of the names. Based on online scuttlebutt alone, it was hard to assess whether they were law-abiding businesses or crooks. Andy had annotated the list with notes about their legal goings-on, which gave a better indication.

There was no implication that the Church of the Early Bright was involved in smuggling, even among its online critics, but Andy had made notes about the feds trying to take away their tax-exempt status because they ran so many profitable businesses. Another client had its business license suspended and then reinstated during a state tax investigation, which is definitely something the accountant, Abner, would be involved in. Next to the entry for a cigar shop, Andy had noted:

> Not really a cigar shop. Sells cannabis. Had three locations shut down by the city for not having permits.

The spreadsheet with Abner's location history was much larger, and extremely detailed, with thousands of rows of data dating back months. Andy had formatted it so that clicking on the cell with the numeric location record brought up a map. He was such a talented guy.

Studying his movements with the list, Abner spent most of his time at his office and at a hotel nearby, which must be where he was sleeping. Other points were storefronts in Hollywood and on the Westside, some of which aligned directly with his clients, the degenerate church and the fake cigar store. As Andy had said, dude ate out a lot, and most of the links brought up restaurants. Every few days Abner went to the apartment in NoHo. Whatever the girlfriend was angry about, it wasn't neglect—he spent several nights a week there.

Andy had highlighted the Albuquerque trips. Abner went to LAX early in the morning, disappearing for a few hours, then surfaced again at the airport in Albuquerque. That was logical, as Andy said the fitness tracker worked with his phone, so it wouldn't record his location when it was in airplane mode. In Albuquerque he made only one stop, and Andy was right—from the street view, it looked like a bar, a lone modern structure built in faux-adobe style, surrounded by an acre of parking. The marquee read LIVE WIRE.

Checking review sites, only a dozen or so users had rated the place, giving it three and a half stars, and only one had bothered to weigh in with words:

Small casual pub with standard brews on tap.

That didn't sound commensurate with an ostentatious fellow like Abner. If he did own the place, he was definitely hiding something.

Flights to Albuquerque weren't that expensive, he found, checking the fares. It was pointless to do that now, as he wasn't even sure he'd need to go. Setting aside his keyboard, he rubbed his eyes and sat there for a minute, eyes closed, focusing on his breathing. There was no way to speed up the recovery from a hangover. How fucking stupid was that, getting so blotto that he'd lost most of the day?

He started awake when keys rattled in the office door. Max stepped in, wearing his gray suit, open at the collar. Slater swung his boots off the desk and got up out of his chair, wiping the drool off his chin with his shirtsleeve.

"Whoa," Max said, pausing to assess him. "You look like hell."

"I fell asleep."

"On Skid Row?"

"I'm kind of working a hangover."

"Have you eaten?"

"Not really."

"You need greasy food," Max said. "I just came in to get some cash. Let's go to that bar where you can eat."

"Sure," Slater said, and stepped into the outer office while Max squatted in front of the safe behind Slater's desk.

Once Max had the safe open, he took some bills from the stash and jotted down details of the withdrawal on the outside of the envelope. Slater stood in the hall and waited for Max to lock up, and they rode the elevator down to the lobby and headed across the street. The parking lot was clearing out, and Max's matte-gray

Challenger, its windows tinted dark, was parked near the Thunderbird.

Max drove them the few blocks to the original downtown, lined with century-old office blocks, and parked at a meter. Odd for a pub but fitting with the neighborhood demographic, the place they were going served cheap drinks and vegan pub food.

As they walked in, Max said, "Hair of the dog?"

"Maybe just a beer," Slater said, and found a table.

Max returned a minute later, two pints of lager in hand, setting them on the table and sliding onto the other chair. "The food will be up in a minute."

Slater sniffed gingerly at the glass, relieved that the yeasty aroma didn't make him want to retch.

"So you were out with a guy?" Max said, after he'd tapped his glass against Slater's.

"I was home alone," Slater said.

"Ouch." Max winced and drank a slug of beer.

"How's your window-shade job going?"

"I wound it up today. The husband is not happy."

"They never are."

"I'm glad to be done with it," Max said. "I just have to pay some vendors."

"So why would a sleazy LA accountant own a bar out of state?"

"Bars are a cash business."

"So what?"

"If you have a bunch of money you can't explain, you put it in the till at the bar. 'Wow, we had a really good month.' You pay your taxes on it, and then it's clean money."

"Interesting," Slater said. "This guy works for lowlifes, so maybe he's helping them launder their income."

"What kind of lowlifes?"

"I'm not sure about all of them, but there's a pot business, and the Church of the Early Bright, and some guy everyone says is a gang kingpin."

"One bar isn't big enough to handle underworld-scale money," Max said. "Plus the gangs have their own fronts. They wouldn't need his."

"I know the church doesn't need his help either. I overheard one of them tell this guy as much. They're smuggling something out of the country through Fort Lauderdale and the Bahamas."

"That would be cash or guns."

"That's what I thought," Slater said. "The churchman talked about an onward flight from the Bahamas, and the Caribbean is full of no-questions-asked banks."

"They wouldn't need their accountant to

process their dirty money in Albuquerque, then."

"So the bar is for this guy to hide his own illicit income. It's not for his clients."

"That makes the most sense," Max said. "Maybe he's helping out the small clients, but not the big guys."

"When you work for crooks," Slater said, "you start to act like a crook yourself."

A woman with a stained green apron set a tray on their table, offloading a pair of veggie dogs with grilled peppers and vegan cheese. Starting into it, Slater realized Max was right—the heavy greasy food felt like the best thing right now for his aching body.

After he polished off his dog, Max wiped his hands. "If gangs are involved, tread carefully."

Slater nodded, sipping at his beer. "I'm not sure how far I'm going to dig. Abner is still in business, so he's clearly outsmarted the regulators. What could I possibly find that they missed?"

SEVEN

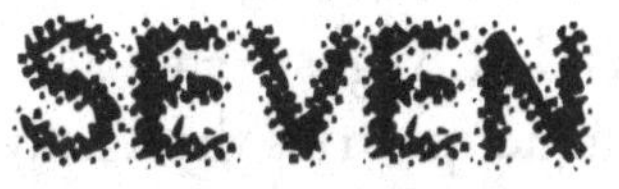

Max dropped him at the curb in front of their office. The building was quiet, the factories shuttered for the night. Slater sat at his computer and stared at it, but he just couldn't focus. Even trying to read the screen was nauseating.

Pulling out his phone, he dialed Marisol, and got her voice mail. "Call me," he told the machine.

Sometime later a buzzing sound woke him from a doze. He was still in his chair, head lolling toward his chest. It was his phone, vibrating on the desktop. Scooping it up, he saw that it was Marisol.

"What do you need?" Slater answered.

"You called me," she said.

"Right." He struggled to remember why. "Did

Abner ever talk about owning property out of state?"

"Not to me. What kind of property?"

"Does he ever travel out of town for business?"

"He never did that when we were together, but we've been living apart for a while now."

"When did he move out?"

"At the end of August," she said.

The Albuquerque trips that Andy had uncovered predated that. Abner was keeping Marisol in the dark.

"What have you uncovered?" she said.

"I'm not sure yet. I'll let you know when I know more."

"Did you tell him that I know about his girlfriend?"

"When I saw him today," Slater said.

"How did he react?"

"He said it wouldn't matter in the divorce."

"We'll see about that," she said, her tone sharp. "I'm half tempted to go to the club and confront him."

"Why would he be at your club at this hour?"

"Not now—tomorrow. That's his club afternoon. He always clears his schedule, and I always avoid the place because I know he's there."

"My advice is to stay away from him. I might know more in a day or two."

"Thank you, Slater," she said. "You're the only

person I can trust right now."

That didn't sound very smart, he thought, ending the call. But it also didn't ring true.

Pushing himself up out of his chair, he flicked off the lights and locked the office, then went down to his car. The lot was almost empty, and Slater climbed into the Thunderbird and drove to his place. It was relatively early, but he needed to crash.

Climbing up the stairs to his apartment, breathing hard, he found a box sitting in front of his door. A floor fan. Conrad. At least he hadn't broken in again.

Carrying it into the kitchen, he pulled it out of the box, and knelt with it on the scuffed and cracked linoleum. He'd need a screwdriver to attach the base. Those were in the garage, but he could not face walking down there again. Every muscle, every joint ached, and his head felt like it was caught in a vise. Collapsing onto his butt, he leaned back against the kitchen counter, his face in his hands.

"Fuck," he roared, and pounded his head with his palms. He'd lost a whole fucking day.

For a minute he sat there with his eyes closed, just breathing, then pulled out his phone and called Andy, who picked up after a couple of rings.

"Can you take me to one of your stupid meetings?" Slater said.

"You want AA, not NA," Andy said. "I can find you an AA meeting."

"I'm not going in cold. I just want to check it out, sit and listen, see what it's like. Is it that different?"

"Sure, I can take you. There's a few every day. The one I usually go to is right near here, on Sunday."

"That works."

"Where are you?" Andy said.

"On the kitchen floor. I mean, I'm at my place."

"Is it bad?"

"Yeah."

"You need somebody there?"

"I just need to sleep. I'll call you in a day or two."

"Don't go cold turkey," Andy said. "You might get the DTs."

"I wondered about that."

"Just go easy."

Slater ended the call and then loosened his laces, kicking off his boots and dragging himself to his feet. On the counter was the fifth he'd bought just yesterday, with a startling volume missing. No wonder he felt like he'd been run over. Cracking it open, he poured half an inch in a tumbler and then slammed it, grimacing at the nauseating burn.

In the bedroom he dropped his clothes on the floor and crawled into bed.

———•———

It was cold when he woke, and he felt jittery, and his head ached, but it was better than yesterday. It was time to do some freaking work, and put the lost time behind him. He got up to pee, shivering in the cold air, then went back to bed, under the warm covers, and lay there for a while, thinking about how he could find out what Abner was up to without pissing off his shady clients. He wasn't about to walk into the Church of the Early Bright and ask what they were shipping to the Bahamas, or start asking questions about money at a pot shop.

Fiber, he remembered. The Durham Building was having fiber installed, and a truck had been parked there yesterday. He could see the loopy laser-beam logo, but what was the company's name? Letting his mind drift, defocusing, it came to him: Willowbrook Fiber.

Grabbing his phone from the bedside table, he looked up the company and dialed the number, glad to get a human being on the other end.

"My name is John Slade," Slater said, "and I have a dental practice on the fifth floor of the Durham Building. Are you still working on the wiring?"

"We cleared out of there yesterday," she said, impatient. "Our part is all done. You have to talk to the internet providers now. We just run the cables."

Next Slater called Max, and when he picked up, said, "Do you have some time for a two-man job?"

"I'm around today."

"Good—bring your blue coveralls and a stepladder."

"We'll take my pickup?"

"That would be perfect," Slater said, and ended the call.

The tech that Slater used, hardware and software for tracking and surveillance and other stealthy research, mostly came from the Russians in Glendale, and he texted Svetlana now:

Can I drop by today to pick up some gear?

Her response soon buzzed his phone:

Visit me anytime. Here until 7.

Me, Slater thought. That meant her brother was still out of the picture. At one point she'd told him that Igor had gone "away," but English wasn't her first language, and Slater wasn't sure whether she meant he was away traveling, or away in prison somewhere—and he didn't want to ask. If Igor was locked up, it was for something other than selling illicit tech, because Svetlana was still in business.

Climbing out of bed, he went to the kitchen and found a ripped-open box of Pop-Tarts. There weren't a lot of vegan snacks on the racks at the liquor store, but some ersatz food was incidentally vegan, like these things. After he ate one, the sugar perked him up, and he started to feel almost normal.

Before he got dressed, he opened the cabinet under the bathroom sink and squatted in front of it, reaching up under the back of the basin, feeling around for the plastic freezer bag he'd wedged in there. It was dusty when he pulled it out, and he shook off a scurrying silverfish. Inside was a thick bundle of hundreds. It would be smarter to keep them in the safe at the office, but it wasn't always convenient to get there when he needed resources. Counting out two grand, he sealed the bag again and reached back under the sink, ramming it tightly into place.

Once he was dressed, he pocketed the cash and went down to his car. The drive to Glendale was slow in the morning traffic, but eventually he pulled up in front of the building where Svetlana ran her business. The tan-pink paint was peeling around the doorway, and metal mesh obscured the windows. The sagging awning above was marked GLENDALE EASTERN IMPORTS.

No one ever used the front door, as far as Slater knew. It was probably nailed shut. Climbing out of the Thunderbird, he walked around to the alley and pushed the bell at the heavily fortified back door, looking into the security camera above and flashing a smile.

Soon the door buzzed open. Waiting for him in the little anteroom was one of Svetlana's staff, a ruddy lanky guy in a dark suit. He gestured for Slater to spread his feet, wordlessly, maybe because he spoke little English, or maybe because they didn't really need to talk. The guy frisked him, a bored expression on his face, although he wasn't shy about thoroughly checking Slater's crotch. Finally he turned and opened the inner door by swiping his wrist at a reader. Svetlana had told him they'd all had RFID tags implanted for that purpose.

The lock snapped open, and Slater followed the suit into the cavernous workroom. It took a moment for his eyes to adjust to the low light. Benches along the walls were cluttered with electronics and tools, and the air was redolent of machine oil and hot plastic. Svetlana was perched on a stool at the workbench along the back wall. In her fifties, she was curvy, filling a loud print top that showed her ample cleavage when she spun around, rattling off a greeting in Russian.

"*Izvinte,*" Slater said. "I haven't been studying."

"That's OK," she said, her accent flattening the vowels, and smiled. "It's good to see you."

"How's Garik?" Slater said, moving closer. He was almost afraid to ask, as Svetlana had practically insisted that they get together. Presumably her nephew and Slater were the only gay guys she knew.

"You didn't hear from your friend Matías?" Svetlana said, frowning. "They are together these days all the time."

"I'm so glad to hear that." Matías wasn't a friend, just someone he'd hooked up with once. Slater had set him up with Garik so that he wouldn't have to sleep with Garik again himself, which he would have done out of obligation, with the risky consequence of getting personally entangled with Svetlana's family.

"It's not the usual way where we come from," she said, "but we can adapt to the local culture. And he's happier than I've ever seen him."

"Say hello from me," Slater said. With any luck it wouldn't blow back on Slater when things ended badly, and romances usually did just that.

"What can we do for you today?" Svetlana said.

"I need some really small cameras. Wireless."

"Where are you putting them?"

"In a drop ceiling, pointing downward."

"What is a drop ceiling?"

"Lightweight tiles, suspended in a metal frame. About this big," he said, holding up his hands and explaining it.

Svetlana soon nodded. "You'll drill through the paper panel for the lens?"

"Whatever the tiles are made of, yeah. It's so light that I'm sure it's permeable."

"It's a kind of paper," she said firmly. Sliding off her stool, she added, "Give me a minute," then disappeared through an inner door.

Slater looked around at the space. So many components—circuit boards, plastic housing, spools of wire.

When Svetlana returned, in her hands was what looked like a stubby black pencil with a wire connecting it to a book-size black box.

"This one might work," she said. "It has a large battery, good for about a week."

Slater took it from her, looking it over. The battery case was heavy, but the lens was miniscule.

"It's the perfect size," he said. "It won't be noticed."

"Don't forget to activate it before you install it," she said, showing him the recessed switch on the battery case. "Once it connects to the cell network, it will show up on your account."

Those account subscriptions must be lucrative for her, as Slater paid for them even when he wasn't doing surveillance. It was well worth it, though—Svetlana's tech, especially the trackers, had saved him many hours of following people around, tailing vehicles, all-night stakeouts. The best part was that her stuff never crapped out or acted buggy. The software was clunky and hard to understand sometimes, but it was sturdy and robust.

"Sweet," Slater said, turning it over in his hands. "How much?"

"Four hundred for this unit. That includes account access."

"I need two of them. Can you cut me a deal?"

Not missing a beat, she said, "Special price for a loyal customer. Seven hundred for the pair."

"That works."

"I'll get the other one," she said, and went out, soon returning with a second identical unit.

Sitting at the workbench again, Svetlana examined the device and then tapped at her computer. Gesturing for him to hand her the other one, she read the label on the bottom of the battery case, then typed on her keyboard. Her screen had a privacy filter, so from his angle Slater could only see diffuse colorful blobs.

"You're connecting them to my account?" Slater said.

"That's right." She rose and put both cameras into a brown paper bag with string handles.

Grinning, Slater pulled out his cash and

peeled off the C-notes, folding them lengthwise and setting them on the workbench. If only the legit tech industry were so efficient and reliable.

Svetlana scooped up the cash, quickly riffling through the bills. "Both units are fully charged." She handed him the bag.

"*Balshoye spasiba,*" Slater said, which elicited a cackle, and the door lock clicked open as he approached it, walking through the anteroom and pushing out into the bright daylight in the alley.

Back around at the Thunderbird, he set the cameras in the trunk and then drove downtown on the 5. In the lot across from their building, Max's little pickup, an early '70s Courier, was parked along the fence, a stepladder lashed to the side of the bed with bungees and a cable lock. The pickup's green paint job was mottled with age, and it had a few dents, but overall it was a sweet little ride. It even had classic blue-and-yellow tags, battered and bent enough that they had to be originals.

From his trunk Slater pulled out the paper bag with the cameras and the duffel bag containing his coveralls, adding to it a couple of screwdrivers and a pair of pliers from his toolbox. When he got up to the office, Max was at his desk, a pair of blue coveralls that matched Slater's draped over the chair in front of it.

"So what are we up to today?" Max said,

looking up as Slater came in.

From the paper bag he pulled out one of Svetlana's cameras and handed it to Max, then explained his plan. Max studied the device, running a fingernail along the side of the stubby camera.

"There are sharp little grooves around the housing," Max said. "It won't slip out of whatever it's mounted in."

"Svetlana thinks of all the angles."

"Should we get dressed here? I wonder if it's a problem that the parking guys see us dressed like plumbers."

"No one gives a damn what we look like or what we do," Slater said.

"Unless we get popped, and then they're all over it."

"We're not going to get popped."

In his own office, Slater pulled on his coveralls and zipped them up, then put the cameras into the duffel bag. Max was already in the front office and dressed the same.

"You put on work boots," Slater said. "So smart."

"Blue-collar guys don't go to work in derbies. I keep these in the pickup."

Following Max out, Slater flicked off the lights and locked the door.

As they walked up on the Courier, Slater said,

"I love this truck. Don't ever leave the keys lying around—you'll never see it again."

Max chuckled and climbed in, reaching across to unlock the passenger door. The little truck had pep but rode rough, the sturdy Japanese engine revving with a high-pitched buzz. Slater gave him directions to the Durham Building, and Max pulled into the underground garage, backing into a stall at a wall near the exit.

From his duffel bag, Slater pulled out two painter's caps, handing one to Max. "There's a security camera in the front office, but not in Abner's office."

"I'll keep my head down," Max said, pulling it on, and then climbed out.

Max unlocked the stepladder and lifted it out, leaning it against the truck.

"I'm not sure this looks right," Slater said, lifting the duffel bag, "but the cameras won't fit in my pockets."

"I'm with you—it doesn't fit. How about this?" Unlocking the cargo box in the bed of the pickup, he heaved out a red plumber's toolbox.

"Much better," Slater said, and they spent a minute transferring the cameras into it.

"Do you have an awl?" Max asked.

"How about a sharp screwdriver?"

"That'll work. Those tiles are usually so light you could poke your finger through them."

Slater carried the ladder and Max took the red toolbox as they went toward the elevators.

"You'll have to do the talking," Slater said. "The receptionist knows me. I'll wait in the hall, and once you're in Abner's office, you can open his back door."

Once they were on Abner's floor, Slater set the ladder against the wall outside the office.

"I'll see you around back," Max said, knocking on Abner's door and pushing his way inside, toolbox in hand.

Slater waited in the hallway, at the corner where it turned a right angle. From here he could see the door to the front office and also Abner's back door, and he could quickly duck out of sight of either one.

Max was the best guy to sweet-talk the receptionist—he wasn't hot, or even handsome, but he knew how to talk to straight women. Exactly how he managed it was mystifying, but they responded to his charm.

Max came out of the office, minus the toolbox, and when he caught sight of Slater, stepped toward him.

"Change of plans," Max said quietly, glancing up the hall. "It's not a woman on the reception desk—it's a bored-looking guy. He says I can't get into the boss's office."

"Why not?"

"I didn't ask. Maybe I can go back in and insist."

"If the woman's not there, I'll come in with you," Slater said.

"What about the security camera? If they already know you, they'll recognize you."

"Most people don't look at the footage unless an incident happens."

"That's kind of what we're doing," Max said. "We're an incident."

"I'll keep my hat on low over my eyes," Slater said. "It'll be fine."

Picking up the stepladder and pulling the brim of his hat lower, Slater followed him back into the office. At the reception desk was a slightly built twenty-something guy, his jet-black hair carefully coiffed. His royal-blue dress shirt looked like it had been ironed. He glanced at Max but spent more time subtly looking over Slater.

"When we were here before, there was a woman on the desk," Slater said.

"We're both part-time," he said, and smiled affably.

"I'll need to get into the panel right behind you," Max said.

"I thought the other guy put the wires closer to the wall," he said, but he rolled out of the way, not rising from his chair.

Max pulled the ladder open, positioning it in the middle of the chair mat. With the guy watching Max, Slater stepped sideways, so Max would be between him and the security camera when he climbed up the ladder. The receptionist swiveled his chair around to look at Slater.

"What's your name, son?" Slater asked, eyeing him.

"Nolan," he said.

That was such an Anglo name, even though he looked Latin, and his dialect was middle-class. Max stepped over to his toolbox, which he'd left on the floor in front of the magazine table. Flipping it open, he pocketed a screwdriver, then went back to the ladder and started up.

Before Nolan could shift focus back to Max, Slater said, "You're certainly more charming than that other one."

Nolan blushed and shifted in his chair. "I thought the fiber installation was done with."

"We found a dead spot when we were testing the lines. We need to check a couple of splitters in your ceiling."

Behind Nolan, Max gingerly pressed up on a ceiling panel, popping it out of its frame.

"So do you have much of a commute to get here?" Slater said, folding his arms.

"I live in Huntington Park, so I take the train," Nolan said.

"Lucky for Huntington Park," Slater said, holding his gaze.

Nolan laughed, his eyes bright. "Do you flirt with people in every office you go into?"

"I never go into offices where there are guys like you."

Max came down the ladder, and Slater dipped his head to avoid the security camera. Stepping over to his toolbox, Max squatted, his back to Nolan, and opened it again, taking out one of the cameras.

"Let me switch it on," Slater said.

"What is that?" Nolan asked.

"It's a leak detector."

Taking the camera for a moment, Slater turned over the battery housing, searching for the miniscule switch Svetlana had shown him, and slid it on with his fingernail. Max headed back up the ladder, and Slater resumed his position, with Max's bulk blocking his view of the security camera.

"Fiber-optic cables can leak?" Nolan asked, frowning.

"Not really," Slater said. "It's just the jargon we use for a technical thing. A leak means signal attenuation. So what do you do when you're not guard-dogging for an accountant?"

"I'm not really a guard dog. I just handle the phone calls."

Above him, Max was working a hole into the ceiling panel, and a thin stream of dust was dropping toward the floor, sparkling as the particles caught the light. As he started to twist the pencil-thin camera lens into the hole, Nolan glanced up at him, and Slater spoke to pull his attention away.

"I assume you've got a boyfriend or a husband. Otherwise I'd totally ask for your number."

Nolan flashed that beautiful smile again. "Why would you think I've got a boyfriend?"

Slater put his hands on his hips. "Guys who look like you don't stay single for long."

Nolan looked away, a smirk on his lips, cocking his head and twisting sideways in his chair, then twisting back. "You are such a flirt, fiber guy."

"The name is Slater."

Avoiding his gaze was just part of the game. Slater could tell he was interested, and he knew that twinkies liked to be pursued.

Pulling out his phone, Slater said, "Don't break my heart, Nolan. What's your number?"

"I'd hate to give you a coronary," Nolan said, and started reciting it.

Glancing up at Max, Slater saw the camera was in place, and he was repositioning the ceiling tile.

"Slow down, Seabiscuit," Slater said. "My fingers are trembling from the excitement."

Nolan guffawed, then told him the number again. Above him the ceiling tile dropped into place. Even from here Slater could see where the camera lens was, a darker spot on the mottled gray-and-white panel. But it wasn't obvious, and no one was going to notice it unless they decided to study the ugly ceiling behind the receptionist's desk.

"Done," Max said, descending the ladder.

"Was it leaking?" Nolan said, swiveling around to face Max.

"We need to get into the back room too," Slater said, gesturing to Abner's office door.

"No can do," Nolan said, shaking his head. "It's locked when the boss is out, and I don't have a key."

"Seriously?" Slater said. "It's just two minutes' work."

"I was here the day your other crew ran fiber in this office," Nolan said. "They didn't work in the boss's office at all. Are you sure your wires are even in there?"

"Above the ceiling it's all connected space," Max said. "But we can come back when the tenant is around. We have other stuff to work on."

"He'll be here Monday," Nolan said.

Max folded the ladder and carried it over to the red toolbox, tossing the screwdriver into it.

"Hold on," Nolan said. He had picked up his

cell phone and was gazing at the screen. "You may be in luck. The boss is on his way up. He just texted me to remind him to renew his parking pass. That means he's downstairs in the garage. The attendant probably bugged him about it."

"It'll have to wait," Slater said. "We have to go." He took the ladder from Max and moved toward the door.

"He'll be here any second," Nolan said. "You won't have to wait long."

"No time," Slater said, and paused at the door to fix him with a smoldering gaze. "Bye, Nolan."

EIGHT

ax followed him into the hallway, and Slater hustled toward the stairwell, listening for the elevators. If Abner stepped off, Slater could do a one-eighty, but that was risky—there wasn't much hallway beyond the back door to Abner's office. Why had he just assumed the guy would be gone all day? He should have checked that stupid fitness tracker page. It would have shown him on his way here. Ducking into the stairwell, he sighed in relief, and took a few steps down, resting the ladder on a stair. Max stood on the landing and let the door close behind him.

"I'm so glad Abner pesters his staff by text," Slater said. "If he'd just walked in, he would have recognized me. That would have been a freaking disaster."

"Nobody's going to the hoosegow today," Max said. "I get why you don't want to run into the accountant, but he doesn't know me. I can go back and work in his office."

Slater shook his head. "Way too risky. He'll know there's no fiber cables up there, and even if you got up the ladder, he'd watch you like a hawk."

"That makes sense. So if you're walking down, maybe I'll take the gear on the elevator."

At that moment the door behind Max flew open, and a guy with a sharp haircut and a lustrous gray silk suit walked in.

"Excuse me," he said pointedly.

Max moved aside but scowled as the guy stepped around him.

"What's wrong?" the guy asked, turning back to Max. "Did you eat too much?" Heading down the steps, he glanced at Slater and muttered, "Fricking foreigners."

Slater swung his boot as the guy passed and tripped him, with his free hand adjusting his trajectory by shoving his shoulder. Twisting sideways and tumbling down a few steps on his butt, he sprawled against the wall at the next landing. Dazed, he picked himself up and swatted dust off his pants, then looked up at Slater, wide-eyed, breathing hard.

"What's wrong?" Slater asked. "Did you trip?"

Not responding, the guy limped down the next half flight, disappearing from view. The sound of the door on the floor below swinging open and slamming shut again resounded in the stairwell.

Slater climbed the few steps to hand the ladder to Max, who had a wry grin on his face. "I'll take the stairs."

Trotting down to the lobby, he didn't pass anyone. Once he was in the garage, keeping his head down, he glanced around for Abner's peroxide pomp and green suit, but no one was in sight.

At the truck, Max gave him the second camera, then took a minute to lock the tools in the cargo box and lash the stepladder to the side.

Once they were driving up the ramp into the bright daylight, Max said, "You certainly know how to lay it on thick. How did you know that kid was gay?"

"The way he checked me out when I walked in."

"He didn't check me out."

"How do you know? He probably did. You're just not tuned into it unless it's a woman."

"Maybe," Max said, checking the traffic as he turned onto Wilshire. "I guess that's kind of flattering."

"So that didn't go the way I'd planned," Slater said, looking out at the city rolling by.

"Still, you got one camera in there."

"You're right. Maybe I'll learn something from watching the front desk."

Max parked the Courier in the lot across from their building, and once they were upstairs, they each spent a minute changing out of the coveralls. Once his were rolled up in his duffel bag again, Slater sat at his desk and pulled up the Russian camera interface on his computer. The device was already connected, and he clicked on the thumbnail image, a wide-angle shot of the reception desk and the carpet, to get a live view.

The video feed showed the top of Nolan's head, the natty blue shirt, and at the side of the frame, the office computer.

"You did it, buddy," he called to Max.

"Did what?" Max said from his office.

"The camera angle is perfect."

Max came in and stood behind him, looking at the screen. "Right on. I was just guessing at how to position the thing."

"It couldn't be better."

"Can you read what's on the screen?"

"I should be able to zoom in, but it might take a minute to figure that out."

"You should just learn Russian," Max said, and chuckled, stepping out again.

In the video feed, the computer screen was an oversaturated bright blur. He wanted to zoom in, but the controls around the image were a jumble of broken English and Cyrillic. Svetlana and her crew built the hardware in her workshop, and they mostly spoke English well, but he suspected that she outsourced writing the software to people in Russia.

Combing through the menus and options, eventually he found a control labeled "зум," which let him get closer to Nolan's computer screen. He positioned the image so the keyboard was visible too, then adjusted the brightness, bringing the contents of the screen into focus.

Nolan was looking at men's dress shoes, scrolling through a list of them, oxfords and derbies and slick Italian styles, occasionally clicking on images. That was pointless to watch, so Slater studied the controls again, setting the software to record when there was motion at the keyboard. Hopefully that was going to work, he thought, gazing at his screen.

In his pocket his phone buzzed, and he pulled it out to find a text from Della, his handler at the insurance company where he got most of his work:

Drop by when you get a minute.

Marisol's prying wasn't keeping him so busy that he couldn't take on a job from Della. Even if it was something he couldn't do, he didn't want Della to forget about him.

Her office was nearby, in the Financial District, and Slater locked his computer and went down to his car, navigating the already congested Friday traffic. Pulling into the garage under the tower where Cudahy Mutual's offices were, he handed his keys to the valet, then rode the elevator up to the thirty-fourth floor.

Nobody was on the reception desk, and the place felt quiet. When he walked back to Della's office, her door was open, and Slater rapped on it and stepped in, taking in the sweeping view out the windows behind her desk, the hazy metropolis stretching to the horizon.

"You're the only one working on Friday afternoon?" Slater asked her.

In her fifties, Della was still shapely, showing some cleavage today in a tight sweater, her hair sprayed into place.

She beamed at the sight of him. "People tend to clear out early for the weekend."

"Must be nice." Slater dropped into a chair. "What have you got for me?"

"It's not a job," Della said, her brow furrowing. "I got a complaint about you."

"Mother fucker," Slater said. "That little weasel."

"It sounds like you already know who called. He threatened to sue Cudahy Mutual for harassment."

"That shit-heel has nothing to do with Cudahy Mutual."

Della raised a hand. "Slater, I'm not worried. People who sue don't announce it beforehand, and people who threaten to sue aren't pragmatic enough to actually do it."

"Good point," Slater said, and sighed.

"I just wanted to give you a head's up."

"I should have dick-punched him when I had the chance."

"You're cute when you're angry," Della said, raising an eyebrow.

Slater grinned at her. "Most people don't think so."

"Don't sweat this guy. You rattled his cage. Don't let him rattle you back."

"That's excellent advice." Slater rose. "I'm glad you're so level-headed about it."

Della leaned back in her chair. "Such a pretty boy. I can't believe you're dick-exclusive."

"It's nice to be appreciated, Della," Slater said flatly, "but it's the *d* for me."

"I think about you sometimes."

"You should think of me as a wrong guy," he said, holding her gaze, then waved as he left, walking back to the elevator.

It wasn't often that he got called "pretty." Hopefully he'd still get work from her if she changed her mind about that assessment.

Once he had his car back from the valet, he drove up the ramp to the street. Fuck Abner for threatening him through Della. Did he really think that would scare him off? Now he really wanted to double down on digging into this trash bag, and to do that, he needed to talk to Nolan. Tapping at his phone, he dictated a text:

Finished work? Can I buy you dinner?

Nolan's response came as Slater braked for the next red light:

Just locking up. Meet me around here?

Slater texted him the name of a *bibimbap* joint a few blocks from the Durham Building, then turned onto Wilshire, heading west.

The place was in a strip mall, and Slater pulled into the narrow lot and parked out front, close to the street. In the corner, by the sidewalk, a short *Thevetia* was blooming in riotous yellow, incongruous with the concrete and asphalt of the dense neighborhood, and he admired it as he walked inside.

People ate early on Friday, it seemed, as the place was busy. Slater got a table with a view of the entrance, and while he was waiting for Nolan, pulled out his phone. If he was going to figure out what Abner was trying to scare him away from, he needed to look into that bar, the Live Wire.

Airfares to Albuquerque for tomorrow weren't actually insane, he saw, and he booked flights that would give him a few hours to do some research. Next he rented wheels from an outfit that would bring the car to him at the curb. It cost a lot more than going to a rental counter, but he wasn't going to have time to mess around.

Nolan walked into the restaurant and looked around, his expression uncertain, but when he spotted Slater he smiled and came over, hanging his backpack on the back of the chair and sitting across from him.

"You're very forward," Nolan said. "But I'm glad you called."

"I'm glad you came."

The waitress handed them menus, and Nolan flipped his open. "I don't really know Korean food."

"Do you just want to have what I'm having?" Slater said. "Rice and tofu and veggies."

"Perfect," Nolan said, folding the menu and waving to the waitress.

Slater ordered for them both, adding, "Hold the egg, yeah?"

Once she'd gone, Nolan asked, "Why no egg?"

"I'm vegan."

"Cool." Nolan nodded. "I went to a vegan Mexican place in Highland Park. It was pretty good."

The first little dishes of pickled vegetables arrived, and Nolan snapped apart a set of wooden chopsticks.

"So is this a date?" he asked, digging in.

"I don't need a boyfriend," Slater said. "But I really want to see you naked."

Nolan raised his eyebrows. "At least there's no ambiguity with you. My only concern is, guys like you never go for me."

"Let me tell you what's wrong with that statement," Slater said, waving his chopsticks. "One, you don't know me, so you don't know what I go for. Two, don't sell yourself short."

He grinned at that, and Slater watched him eating, deftly working the chopsticks. The guy was young, but he certainly wasn't inexperienced with food.

After they'd both finished, Slater pushed away his bowl. "I live in Westlake. Do you want to come to my place?"

"For the naked thing?"

"If you're up for that."

"Let's go," Nolan said, and scooted out his chair.

Slater paid at the register and followed him into the parking lot, climbing into the Thunderbird and reaching across to unlock the passenger door.

"Sweet rig," Nolan said as he got in.

"It breaks down sometimes," Slater said. "Way more than a new car would. But I love it, so it seems worthwhile."

"Why do you love it?"

"Cars aren't fun anymore," Slater said, swiveling his head to check the traffic as he pulled onto the street. "New ones all look exactly the same. You have to squint and read the logo to figure out what make they are. This one has its own look."

"I can't argue with that," Nolan said, and wound down the passenger window, watching the city go by, resting a hand on top of the door, his elbow jutting out.

Navigating the few blocks to Westlake, Slater pulled into his garage, then unlocked the door into the building and held it for Nolan, who followed him up the stairs. Stepping inside Slater's apartment, he looked around, but didn't seem startled or repulsed. He probably came from an income stratum where this kind of place was the norm.

"Are you trying to put your fan together?" Nolan said, surveying the unboxed pieces on the kitchen floor. He slid off his backpack and set it on the counter.

Stepping up behind him, Slater put his arms around his waist. Nolan leaned into him, and Slater breathed in the scent of his hair, then ran his hands under Nolan's shirt, feeling his belly and his chest. Nolan took a deep breath. Sliding his hands into his pants, Slater found his cock already engorged.

Slater pulled away and led him into the bedroom, unbuttoning Nolan's shirt and sliding it off, draping it carefully on the floor so as not to introduce wrinkles—somebody had taken the time to iron it, after all. Sitting on the edge of the futon, Slater kissed his belly and his chest, nuzzling his delightfully smooth hairless skin. Nolan unbuckled his belt and shoved his pants down, and Slater took him into his mouth, hands on his waist. Nolan moaned as Slater got into it, his fingers in Slater's hair. Suddenly Nolan yelped, and spasmed, and came. Slater hadn't expected that.

Pulling away, Slater sank back on the bed, and grabbed Nolan's arm, guiding him down beside him.

"I didn't mean to come so fast," Nolan said.

Slater ran his fingers through Nolan's hair. "You don't need to apologize for that."

"You got me so turned on." He leaned in and kissed him.

Slater explored his mouth, warm and taut, then pulled away, unbuckling his belt and sliding off his jeans.

"Do you want to fuck me?" Nolan said, meeting his eye and squeezing his swollen cock.

"That doesn't seem like the thing right now," Slater said, and kissed his neck.

"Let me blow you," Nolan said, and shifted to the floor.

Slater gasped as he got into it. The guy knew what he was doing, his mouth firm and confident. It was a real turn-on when he looked up at Slater with those beautiful eyes. Even so, it took him longer to build up to it than it had Nolan, and eventually he came, grunting and arching his back.

Grinning, Nolan climbed on the bed and wrapped an arm across Slater's sweaty chest as he caught his breath.

Slater was close to drifting into sleep when Nolan spoke.

"How long have you worked for the fiber company?"

Slater had almost forgotten about that. "Not long."

"When will they switch over from cable?"

"We just put in the wires. The internet providers do that part. It's up to the tenants, like your boss. He's an accountant, right?"

"So he says."

"Do you do any accounting?"

"I just handle calls and set up appointments," Nolan said, pulling his arm away and shifting onto his back. "He doesn't even need a receptionist, but it makes him look like a bigger entity to have staff. In front of his clients, he calls us his assistants."

"What's he like, the boss?"

"His name is Abner. I'd say he's kind of tacky."

"What does that mean?" Slater said, eyeing him.

"Well, when he meets a client, I have to bring in coffee and these stupid little biscotti, like a waiter. Plus he's kind of lecherous."

"Has he groped you or something?"

"It's the way he looks at me," Nolan said. "Dead-eyed, like he has no soul, but hungry, like he wants to lick me."

"That sounds totally tacky. What kind of clients does he have?"

"Old men, mostly. People like him. I only see them on the way in."

"Why does he have two people in the front office?"

"We each work three days. I'm on Monday, Wednesday, Friday. She does the other three."

"The office is open Saturday?"

"I guess his clients come in sometimes."

"Still, it sounds more like one job, not two."

"He wants part-timers so that he doesn't have to offer benefits or deduct money for taxes. He pays us in cash, like we're day laborers."

"That seems shitty, considering he's an accountant," Slater said. "Do you have another job?"

"I work in a paint store. I have a uniform and everything."

Slater chuckled, and rolled onto his side, wrapping an arm around Nolan's belly, pulling his warm buttocks against his thighs.

———◆———

Sometime later his phone buzzed, waking him. Reaching for his jeans on the floor, he pulled it out and found a text from Andy:

Want to come over?

Slater thumb-typed a reply:

Can't tonight. Talk tomorrow.

He climbed out of bed, not turning on the light.

"Where are you going?" Nolan asked, sleep in his voice.

"I'll be right back."

In the kitchen Slater poured an inch of bourbon into a tumbler and then slammed it, shuddering with nausea after it went down. Rinsing out the glass, he drank some tap water to dilute the smell on his breath. Back in bed, Nolan shifted when he climbed in, folding his knee over Slater.

"I can't believe we're both sleeping," Slater said. "It's like, nine o'clock."

"Can I stay?" Nolan asked softly.

"Of course you can."

Nolan got up and went out, his slender form

silhouetted against the diffuse light from the window in the main room. Slater could hear water running in the bathroom, and Nolan returned a minute later with his backpack in hand. Looking around on the floor for his pants, he pulled out his phone and turned on its flashlight, scanning the wall beside the bed.

"Score," he said, and Slater watched as he dug his phone charger out of his bag and plugged it into the wall socket he'd found, bringing the end of the cable with him as he crawled into bed. As he thumb-typed, the glow of the screen illuminated his face. Finally plugging in his phone and setting it on the carpet, he moved close to Slater again.

It felt good, the proximity to the kid, the warmth. The bourbon was softening his mind now, slowing things down, and he sank back into sleep.

NINE

olan was getting dressed when Slater woke. It was early, he saw, grabbing his phone. That was a relief—he had a flight to catch. It was nice to be lucid and not in pain, he realized, sitting up.

"I wish I could offer you breakfast," Slater said.

"There's a million places on the way to the paint store," Nolan said, buttoning his shirt. "That was fun. Can I call you?"

"I hope you will," Slater said, and got up, following him to the front door.

Nolan turned to kiss him good-bye, and Slater put his hands on his butt, pulling him against his naked body.

"Stop that," Nolan said, and laughed. "You'll make me late."

After he left, Slater locked the deadbolt and went back to bed, relishing the warmth under the covers. He sent Andy a text:

Can I drop by? I'll pay you—what do I owe you?

His reply came a minute later:

$900. I'm here all day.

That boy did not work cheap, but Slater had to admit it was worth it—the information he'd uncovered was extremely valuable.

Dozing a little longer, Slater enjoyed the stillness of the morning, then pushed himself to get up, and get dressed, and head down to his car.

As he crossed the chasm of the 110 freeway into downtown, the street was blocked by barricades, and a couple of traffic cops in tan shirts were waving vehicles onto a cross-street. The traffic slowed to a crawl. He never bothered to use navigation on his short commute, but maybe he should have today. Looking down into the core, a block away he could see a throng of people, some of them holding signs, walking north toward the Civic Center. Doris's protest, he remembered. She was in there with her friends, everybody headed to Grand Park for speeches and shared outrage. The thought of Doris yelling about politics made him grin.

Once he was through the bottleneck, the

traffic sped up, and he parked at his office, trotting across the street in a break between cars.

Abner's office was open today, Nolan had said, and once he was sitting at his desk, he pulled up the interface for the camera he and Max had hidden there. The live feed showed the woman with the dark-rimmed glasses—the top of her head and her shoulders, at least—sitting at the reception desk, doing something with her cell phone. At the side of the page was a long list of clips that had been recorded, starting this morning, probably when the receptionist had arrived. Why were there so many? It had to be about the camera angle, he realized—every time she inadvertently moved in front of the keyboard, it triggered a recording.

Clicking on the file for 8:06 this morning, he saw her drop her oversize handbag in the bottom drawer of her desk, and then settle into her chair and adjust her ample breasts. In the next clip she shook the computer's mouse to wake it up, then typed something, stared at the screen, and typed again.

Rewinding the clip, Slater found the "зум" control and focused on her keyboard, watching her typing. He couldn't see every keystroke, but the website that appeared on her screen was a grid of boxes—a calendar. Rewinding again, he fiddled with the controls until he found the slow-motion function, "замед." Grabbing a pen and a pad from his desk drawer, he wrote down the web address, and then the user name—predictably, "Abner Hart." The password took a little longer to get, and he had to rewind a couple of times, and guess at one of the characters, either a *C* or a *V.*

Pausing the video, Slater opened another browser tab and typed in the website address, using Abner's credentials. The calendar grid appeared—he'd gotten the password right.

"Thank you, Svetlana," Slater said, and poked around Abner's calendar. It was just scheduling software, and had nothing at all to do with his accounting work. That wasn't optimal, but it fit with what Nolan had told him, that the front-desk job was just for reception.

Abner didn't have many appointments marked, never more than two or three in a day, and Fridays were usually blank. Meetings were marked only with surnames—Sanchez, Berger, Wilson. Scrolling through past months, he realized he might be able to figure out who these people were by cross-referencing them with Andy's client research.

Back on the camera page, he watched the rest of the morning's video clips, but the receptionist didn't use the computer again, and didn't do anything even remotely enlightening. Slater checked the time. He could look at all this later. Locking his computer, he squatted in front of the safe, opening it and counting out the cash he needed for Andy, then wrote on the envelope the date and "Marisol Hart case." It was an irresponsible way to keep track of money, he knew that. But Abner paid Nolan the same way, and he was a professional accountant. Maybe it was for the same reason—it didn't create a paper trail. O'Dowd, their new accountant, would definitely not approve. With a twinge of guilt, he remembered he still hadn't finished his expenses list for her.

Stuffing the bills in his pants, he locked the safe, then went downstairs and drove to Andy's, parking in the adjacent surface lot. Andy opened the door, his face breaking into that perfect smile. He wore his usual boxer shorts and a T-shirt, and a few days' stubble darkened his face.

Slater followed him inside and handed him the nine hundred.

"Thanks," Andy said, taking the cash. "How come you never negotiate?"

"I usually do," Slater said. "With other people, at least."

"Why not me?" Andy said, stepping over to his desk and dropping the bills on it.

"I don't know. Maybe because we're sleeping together."

"I inflate my rate because I ... expect to have to discount it," Andy said. "You have to negotiate."

"Next time," Slater said. "Do you want to cuddle?"

"Hell, yes," Andy said, enthusiastic. It was a thing they did, a pattern they'd established, and he loved it as much as Slater did.

Slater dropped into the easy chair under the windows, and Andy sat in his lap, wrapping his arms around Slater's neck. Slater stabilized him with his hands firmly on Andy's waist. Andy moved in to kiss him, lingering in it, then rested his forehead on Slater's. Closing his eyes, Slater leaned into his gentle random muscle movements.

"Are we still on for tomorrow?" Andy said finally, his tone soft.

"Do I have a choice? I figured that once I'd rung that bell, I'd never get out of it."

Andy chuckled. "Why are you suddenly interested in twelve-step?"

"I lost a whole day. I couldn't do anything, couldn't think straight. I woke up with my ex looming over me, two fingers on my neck, checking to make sure I wasn't dead."

"You drunk-dialed him?"

Slater sighed and looked away. "I'm such a fuckup."

"I disagree. But NA is different from what you need."

"AA, I know—people keep telling me that. It just seems so boring."

"Maybe SCA too."

"What's that?"

"Sexual compulsives. It's mostly gay guys."

"I'm not compulsive," Slater said.

"That's not the point. It's like AA, except instead of booze, it's sex that's messing up your life."

"Sex doesn't mess up my life. I have it neatly compartmentalized. I don't take risks, I don't drink beforehand, and I don't fuck tweakers and junkies."

"So there are rules," Andy said. "Just like with your drinking."

Slater closed his eyes and massaged Andy's back. There was nothing he could say to that.

"It's not about sex itself, but the pursuit of it," Andy said. "The time … you spend on it. That's what messes people up."

"Just let me lurk in your meeting," Slater said. "I don't need a lecture."

Andy kissed him again, moving to his cheek, then nuzzled his neck, his stubble rough and scratchy and perfect. Slater breathed in the heady scent of his hair.

"You're hard," Andy said. "Do you want to take this horizontal?"

"You just got through telling me that I'm a sex addict."

"Sex with me doesn't count."

Slater scoffed. "I wish I had the time. I have

a plane to catch. I'm going to check out that bar you found in Albuquerque."

"So I did good?"

"Very good. Nine yards' good."

"You sound like a gangster," Andy said, and kissed him again, then added gently, "Be careful."

Disentangling himself, Slater went back down to his car and headed for the airport. Like everyone, he hated the snarled cluster-fuck of congestion at LAX, the 1960s infrastructure handling twenty-first-century traffic. Eventually he made it into a day lot across from the right terminal, and pulled his earbuds out of the dash. He never used them in the car, but they were useful in crowded public places, to tune out the chaos.

"No carry-on?" the screener asked him as he stepped through the metal detector.

"It's a short trip."

"Keep walking," she said flatly.

Soon he was in the air, his earbuds jammed in tightly. He shook his head when the drink cart came by, even though it was so easy to drink on a plane, when there was nothing else to do. But it didn't fit his booze rules—he wasn't with anyone, it was still daytime, and there was work to be done.

———•———

Cavernous and mostly devoid of life, the terminal in Albuquerque looked more like a train station than an airport. Walking outside, he was struck by how cold it was. He hadn't expected that. What was he thinking? He should have checked on the damn weather. At least it wasn't so cold that he needed to go buy a parka. His phone buzzed in his pants, and when he looked, it was a text from the car rental people, telling him to proceed out to the curb.

Sure enough, when he got there, he spotted a Charger with a guy loitering beside it. It was white, such a bland color for a car, but in the desert, white probably made sense.

"Slater?" the guy said as he walked up.

"That's me."

"Can you show me your receipt?"

The text he'd gotten had a bar code in it, and he pulled out his phone, showing it to the guy, who positioned his own phone over it for a second.

Pulling it back and studying the screen, he said, "You're the guy," and handed Slater the key. "When you come back, lock the key in the car."

"Just park it here again?"

"That's the idea. Have fun."

Climbing in, the Charger's interior was much warmer than outside, and Slater started the engine to get the air blowing. After he adjusted the mirrors, he found the Live Wire bar on his navigation app and popped the transmission into Drive.

The air was so clear here, he saw, once he

was on the freeway. The mountains were sharp and vivid, and probably farther away than they looked. Even in the city the landscape was stark and beautiful, the color palette different than LA, in bright tans, rich reds, and turquoise splashed on buildings and bridges.

The Live Wire was a faux adobe building standing alone in a dusty parking lot, a neon beer logo visible in the front window. Two cars were parked out front, he saw, cruising past, and the fact that the sign was lit meant it was open. Pulling into the lot, he parked behind the building, swinging the Charger around to face the street.

The interior was dark when he stepped inside, and he paused for a moment for his eyes to adjust. The bar ran the length of one wall, fronted by stools upholstered in red vinyl. Beyond that were a few tables, some square, some round, the chairs all mismatched, as if everything came from a flea market. The walls were paneled in dark wood, with a well-worn dartboard in the corner.

At the far end of the bar sat a lone patron, a rail-thin gray-haired guy, hunched over a pint. He looked up briefly as Slater stepped inside. Behind the bar was a middle-aged woman, in a white shirt with a black vest, wispy hair bundled behind her head. Her face was blotchy and deeply lined from way too many years in the sun.

She nodded a perfunctory greeting and

stepped over as Slater took a stool.

"Whatever beer you have on tap," he said, and set a twenty on the bar.

While he waited, he picked up a coaster, a white disk printed in black with LIVE WIRE. Behind the letters ran a thin red line that curled around and terminated under the words, red sparks shooting from its tip. The concept was the same as Willowbrook Fiber's logo—energy unleashed. Looking around the empty bar, that was definitely the wrong metaphor.

Slater dropped the coaster, and the woman set a pint glass on it, then plucked the twenty. When she returned from the register, she had a lot of bills—this was cheap beer.

As she set down his change, Slater said, "This place doesn't seem very busy."

"The lunch crowd is gone, and after that it's only serious drinkers until it gets dark," she said, glancing down the bar at the gray-haired guy.

"Even on Saturday?"

"What you see is what you get," she said.

"Are you the manager?"

"Sorry, hon, we're not hiring."

"I wanted to ask about the owner."

She frowned. "Who are you?"

"I'm an insurance investigator."

"I didn't file any insurance claims. You'll have to talk to whoever did."

"Does Abner come around much?"

Concern flickered in her eyes, and she put her hands on her hips. "Who did you say you work for?"

"I didn't say. So what does this place clear in a week?"

The woman turned toward the doorway that led into the back and shouted, "Ed! Eighty-six." To Slater, she jutted her chin and said, "Go on, get out of here, or I'm calling the cops."

Slater rose and picked up his change, leaving her a dollar, and took a slurp from his watery pint before he walked out.

That had happened fast. The thing about Ed the bouncer lurking in the kitchen was probably just a bluff, but even so, he'd learned something— just the mention of Abner's name had raised her hackles.

As he walked behind the building toward his car, he saw a guy climbing out of a battered old blue Taurus. Dark and with a neat little mustache, he wore the same shirt and black vest as the bartender inside. As he approached the guy, Slater glanced toward the bar to make sure he wasn't being observed. But there was no one around, and not even a window in the back of the building.

"Do you bartend here?" he asked.

He stopped and eyed Slater. "I'm a bar back. I don't think they need anybody right now."

His Spanish accent was slight, so he'd been here a while.

"I'm not looking for work," Slater said. "Do you know the owner?"

"I don't know nothing," he said, his tone guarded.

Digging in his pocket, Slater palmed a twenty, concealing it as he pulled it out, but letting the guy see what it was before reaching toward him. The guy briefly grasped his hand, half slap, half handshake. The bill disappeared.

"I see him once a month," the bar back said quietly, glancing over Slater's shoulder toward the Live Wire. "He comes in for a while and talks to Dolores in the office."

"Dolores is the manager?"

"If you were just inside, she's the one behind the bar."

"The owner is a blond guy, right? Kind of soft?"

The bar back frowned slightly. "I guess that sounds like him."

Slater pulled out his phone and found Abner's website, zooming in on his portrait, then holding it up.

"That's the guy," he said, peering at the screen. "I never seen him in a suit, though."

"You said he comes in for a while," Slater said. "How long?"

He shrugged. "Two or three hours."

"Do you know what the books look like?"

"What books?"

"Accounting—income and expenses."

"The money? I don't know nothing about that. I wash glasses and stack kegs."

Slater nodded. "OK."

"I can tell you one thing—payday is always the day after the owner visits."

"You get paid in cash?"

"Always in cash." Glancing at the bar again, he said, "I should go."

Slater watched him walk toward the Live Wire, then went back to the Charger and pulled out onto the quiet street. The Live Wire was definitely Abner's place, and the employee backed up the fitness tracker data—Abner showed up regularly, right before payday. He had to be injecting cash into it.

A few blocks away, on a stretch of road with mostly empty lots, he pulled over and left the engine running. This town was odd—the freeways were a little busy, but the streets were uniformly quiet. It didn't feel quite like a recession, with failed businesses and broken windows. It was more like there had never been a spark, never a lot going on economically, no energy unleashed.

Checking the clock on his phone, he still had time before he had to show up for the flight back to LA. Opening the hookup app, he found slim pickings. That made sense in a small town. Swiping through, there were even fewer guys, as lots of them were way too far away. But there were some options. Just a couple of miles from him was a gray-haired guy with a wry smile, his face creased by time and the desert. In one of the photos he was wearing a black vaquero hat with a purple ostrich feather in the band. This was the guy. Slater messaged him:

> I have 90 minutes. Your place, and you have to wear the hat.

His reply came quickly, a street address. Grinning at the success, Slater put it into his navigation app.

Pulling up at the place, he killed the engine. It was a low bungalow with cacti and gravel instead of a lawn. A trio of wispy shade trees stood at the side of the yard, maybe piñons, or a close relative. In the driveway was a well-used pickup with those funky turquoise tags.

When he answered the door, the guy was wearing a plaid shirt, and jeans, and the hat, minus the ostrich feather. He smiled at the sight of Slater, the corners of his eyes creasing. His skin had seen a lot of sun, like that woman at the bar.

"That was fast," he said, standing aside to let him in.

Slater stepped into his living room, cluttered

and comfortable, with a weird dome-shaped fire-place in the corner.

"So why am I wearing my hat indoors?" he asked.

"I saw it in your photo," Slater said. "I thought it looked cool."

"Want to try it?" He pulled it off and handed it to Slater.

Its contour was formed to the guy's head, the lining mottled with years of sweat. The wide flat brim was made of heavy black felt. This was the real deal—a working man's hat, not stylized for the movies or product marketing. It would definitely keep the sun off.

"It doesn't quite fit me," Slater said, briefly trying it and handing it back. "It looks good on you, though. It's a Spanish style?"

He tossed it on the coffee table. "I'd call it New Mexico style, but most people around here claim Spanish blood. Where are you from?"

"Is it that obvious that I'm not local?" Slater said. "Is it because I look like a mutt?"

"Everyone's a mutt. My father claimed to be descended from the conquistadors, but not the Indians. How would he know that? You can't unscramble that omelet."

"That makes sense."

"I figured you're not local because I never saw you online before."

Slater stepped closer and took the guy's hands, massaging his leathery palms with his thumbs. "Guess," he said. "Where am I from?"

The guy cocked his head and frowned thoughtfully, squeezing Slater's hands. "Well, you look Latin, but you sound Anglo, and you're pretty impatient, so I'd say, with seventy percent certainty, Los Angeles."

Slater chuckled. "Impatient?"

"You said you only had ninety minutes."

"What's your name?" Slater asked.

"Ken."

"Well, Ken, the clock is ticking." Slater moved closer, meeting his mouth, hard and warm and insistent, tasting of coffee or tobacco or both.

Ken grabbed his butt and pulled him close. "Damn—you're already hard. You want to fuck me with that thing?"

"Oh, yeah," Slater said.

"I'll be right back." Ken pulled away and stepped into the hall.

Slater looked around the room. The blinds were closed—Ken wanted it to happen here. The sofa would work, he decided. It was low and deep and looked comfortable, with a red-striped Navajo blanket draped over it. Slater took his shirt off, unbuckled his belt, and sat down.

Ken returned with condoms and lube, and knelt on the sofa, straddling Slater, sitting on his knees and kissing him again. Unbuttoning Ken's shirt, the skin below his collar and above his elbows was startlingly pale, like he was still wearing an undershirt, and his nipples were tiny. Slater unbuckled his belt, running his hand over Ken's soft pasty belly. Ken was trembling in anticipation, sweat beading on his skin. Slater kissed his neck. Ken rose to slide his jeans off, and Slater did the same, kicking off his boots. When he straddled Slater again, Ken grabbed his raging hard cock.

"Let me put this on you," Ken said, and tore open a condom.

When Slater penetrated him, Ken screwed his eyes shut and arched his back, sinking into it. Ken did most of the work, slowly at first, building up in intensity until he was pounding him. Grabbing his shoulders and straining into him, Slater came with a roar, then pulled him closer, kissing his sweaty chest, his frostbitten nipples.

After a minute, when Slater's breathing had slowed, Ken said softly, "Do you want to smoke me?"

Slater chuckled and said, "Sure."

Shifting onto the floor, he took Ken into his mouth, one palm on his belly, working his other thumb inside him. Ken quickly got hard, responding to Slater's rhythm, and then, grunting and straining, he climaxed.

Slater sat back on the floor, leaning on his

elbows, catching his breath. Ken rose and walked into the back of the house, returning a moment later with a towel, tossing it to Slater. Crouching, Ken picked up the cash and cards and keys that had spilled out of Slater's jeans, stuffing them back in the front pocket.

"Insurance investigator?" he said, looking at one of Slater's cards.

"Keep that, if you want," Slater said. "Look me up if you're ever out my way."

Ken set the card on the coffee table. Dropping onto one end of the sofa, he extended his hand and pulled Slater up beside him. "Maybe you could show me around your town."

"I don't think you'd like it," Slater said, putting an arm around his neck. "My whole apartment would fit inside your living room. And what I do isn't pretty."

"Insurance?" Ken said, eyeing him sidelong. "That just sounds a little dull, not ugly."

"I do bad things," Slater said. "I hurt people."

"We all do that, son. There's no love without pain."

"That's not what I meant."

Ken grinned. "So you're a bad boy?"

Slater nodded. "Real bad."

"You know that only makes you hotter, right?"

Slater scoffed, massaging Ken's neck for a moment, then said, "I should go."

As he got dressed, Ken got up too and waited, pulling on his shirt but not buttoning it. Tying his boots and then rising, Slater took the hat from the table and set it on Ken's head.

"It looks so sharp," Slater said.

"I'm glad it caught your interest."

"What happened to the feather?"

"That's for formal occasions."

Slater nodded. "You should wear this every single day. It's a total dick magnet."

"I do," Ken said, and laughed, then followed Slater to the door as he left.

Driving to the airport, he marveled again at the clarity of the sky, the bright quality of the light, even this late in the day. It was like the vividness setting for reality itself was cranked up a notch. Could he ever live in a place like this, wear a hat like Ken's? He'd need a winter jacket. And what the hell would he do out here? No, LA was in his blood. They'd have to plant him there.

Dusk was encroaching as he pulled up to the curb outside the airport. Finding the message about the rental, he texted back:

Car at curb. Key in visor.

It felt plain wrong to lock the keys inside, but that's what they wanted. As he walked around the front end of the Charger, he said, "Thanks, car," and headed inside.

On the plane, his earbuds jammed in, he thought about the Live Wire. Showing up there once a month, Abner was definitely running money through the place. The books, the payroll, even dealing with vendors could all be done remotely, but injecting cash—that required going in person. But why not buy a business somewhere closer, in California? Maybe there was less regulation, less oversight, lower taxes. Closing his eyes, he pushed it out of his mind and tried to nap.

When they landed at LAX, Slater turned on his phone and texted Marisol:

Can I see you?

Her response came while the plane was still taxiing to the gate:

Drop by the house.

LAX felt like a zoo compared to the serene airport in Albuquerque, and Slater elbowed his way through the crowds, out to the curb through the haze of smokers, and across the roadway to the parking lot. This looked nothing like where he'd parked. It was dark out now, but that wasn't the issue, he realized—this was a completely different terminal. It made sense, as he'd come back on a different airline. Still, this whole place felt like it was purpose-built to waste time.

The structure where his car was parked would

be behind this one, he decided, after standing there for a moment thinking about it. He walked into the dimly lit laneway along the side of the structure, the quiet emptiness almost jarring after the chaos at the curb outside the terminals.

From a doorway in front of him a guy with a bushy beard hurried out of the parking lot, dragging a roller bag into his path. Slater stumbled over it, managing to keep his balance but knocking the bag on its side.

"Idiot," the guy muttered, scowling at him in annoyance, then yanking his bag back onto its wheels and striding away.

"Sure, like that was my fault," Slater called after him.

Longbeard quickened his pace, glancing over his shoulder. Slater knew he should walk away, knew what the parade of shrinks Doris had sent him to through his childhood would say: "Let it go." But they weren't here, and he just couldn't be that guy right now. Loping to catch up, he hooked his boot around Longbeard's shin, and at the same moment pulled back on his shoulder. The technique was meant to dump him on his ass rather than onto his hands and knees. It was a kindness, really—rather than skinned knees and shredded palms, the guy might just walk away with dusty pants. As planned, Longbeard twisted and tumbled onto his butt on the dirty concrete, holding up his forearm in self-defense.

"I'm sorry," he cried, and his bag flopped over, its handle slapping on the concrete.

Slater grabbed his hand and pulled it away, and with his other palm slapped his face, hard.

"Why do you make me do this to you?" he shouted, and slapped him again.

Longbeard twisted away, shielding his face, then got to his feet and staggered a few steps before he looked back, his eyes darting from Slater to his suitcase. Slater had made his point, he decided, and technically the dumb-ass had apologized. Glancing around to make sure they hadn't been observed, he turned his back and went on his way, across a road and into the adjacent parking structure, glancing back once to make sure Longbeard hadn't been stupid enough to follow him.

Once he found his car, he paid the exorbitant hourly rate and crawled into the snarl of traffic, eventually merging onto the 105, finally free of that rat hole and its insane congestion.

TEN

The Thunderbird's headlights illuminated Marisol's oversize house as he drove up, and Slater parked on the street, walking back to ring the bell.

Marisol had a tumbler in hand when she opened the door, barefoot and in dark-green capris, her blouse unbuttoned enough to show several thin necklaces and the fringes of her bra.

"Come in," she said, and led him up to the lounge room with the bar.

The lights were still on in the little garden with the manzanita, but Slater held his tongue about that.

"Scotch?" Marisol said, raising her eyebrows.

"Just a tiny splash. Like half a drink," he said.

She stepped behind the bar, and Slater

watched her pour. Setting the tumbler on the bar top, she refilled her own.

"I like that you drink it neat," he said.

"Why would I alter the flavor of something so divine?"

She smiled and handed him the glass, then sank into an overstuffed easy chair. Slater sat across from her and sipped at the delectable perfect scotch.

"Did you know that Abner owns a bar in Albuquerque?" Slater said.

"I never heard that before," Marisol said, her brow furrowing. "How did you find it?"

"Don't worry about my methods."

"What kind of bar?"

"It's a small place, kind of a dive, and not very busy."

"You went there?"

"Today," Slater said. "I'll send you the address."

"Surely Abner's just a hands-off investor. It must be, what, two days' drive?"

"He flies out, once a month, just for the day."

Marisol sipped her drink, lost in thought. Finally she looked at him. "You're certain that he goes there?"

"One of the employees ID'd him."

"Why does Abner own a bar in Albuquerque?"

"I don't have any evidence, but it seems likely that he's using the place to launder money. Bars work mostly in cash, and if there's a lot of it flowing through, nobody's going to question it."

"How much money?" she demanded. "And where is it coming from?"

"I have no idea."

"Not from his fishy clients," Marisol said, waving her hand. "They do it for themselves. You don't ask the bookkeeper to wash your dirty money."

Slater sipped his scotch, gloriously aromatic and delicious, watching her. She knew exactly what he was talking about, understood it in detail.

"You could only run so much cash through a small business," Slater said, "so you're right, it's not likely for his clients."

"That's important. It means there's money that he's hidden from me. Even without the washing, the bar alone is an asset I never heard of. Can you get more details on what happens with this bar?"

"Maybe. It is an interesting question, why he has money that needs to be hidden. I'll see what I can find out."

Marisol rose. "Do you need another payment? If you flew out there, you must be racking up expenses."

"You don't have to pay me now," Slater said, rising and pausing to slam the contents of his glass, savoring the burn.

"You like that stuff, I can tell," Marisol said, a smile playing on her lips.

"It's probably the best scotch I've ever had."

She nodded approvingly. "So where are we at, money-wise? Give me a number."

Slater furrowed his brow. "Another two grand so far. We can talk about the next steps in a day or two."

"That's fine."

She walked him to the door, then called after him, "Good night."

Slater glanced back and lifted his palm, and she just stood there, watching him go. Maybe she'd had more to drink than it seemed, or maybe she was just bored. At least she hadn't made a move on him this time. Where was that little weasel of a driver, Randall? He'd acted all protective, so he probably had a crush on her. That kind of guy would alleviate the boredom.

Twisting the key in the ignition, he flicked on his headlights and headed down the hill. Marisol hadn't been at all surprised that Abner was up to something, and she was totally versant in lowlife business practices. She really just wanted details, which meant she knew a lot more than her wide-eyed innocent shtick implied. She was also the only one who had talked about firearms, he remembered. Hopefully he hadn't endangered

Abner's life by ferreting out his illicit scheme at the Live Wire.

As he pulled into his garage, he realized he was tired, his muscles stiff, his eyes dry. Walking into his apartment, he eyed the bourbon, and the unassembled fan on the floor, then stooped to untie his boots, kicking them off by the door. He poured an inch of the beautiful amber into a tumbler and sipped at it, then stretched out on the sofa in the dark, setting the glass on the carpet and loosening his belt. Sure, he'd overdone it the other night, but that didn't mean he had to quit completely. Andy would never let him wriggle out of that meeting, though. He'd screwed himself by even bringing it up.

Taking a mouthful of the bourbon, he relished the burn as it went down. His mind was settling, he could feel it. The world was calming down. But such a limited quantity took him only a few steps down, half a flight. What he longed for was the floor to drop away beneath him, to go into freefall.

Fumbling with his phone, he put on *Sasquatch Search*. That usually helped him get to sleep, numbed his mind. Plus he'd been on goddamn airplanes today for hours and hours, enough to suck the life out of anyone. He should be completely wiped out. It made no sense that he was even awake right now. Draining the tumbler, he put his arm over his eyes and tried to focus on the narrator, following him deep into the woods.

———◆———

Slater woke up in bed, his head clear, his body pain-free. It was weird that he had no memory of getting into bed, even when he wasn't blotto, but here he was, naked and alone. He must have been thoroughly exhausted.

It was still mid-morning, he saw, checking his phone. Enjoying the warmth under the covers and knowing the floor and everything else outside this bed were going to be cold, he lay there for a while, thinking about the Live Wire, Marisol abandoning her naive act, Ken and his boss vaquero hat. Abner's work. He needed to get a look at that, and see where the money was coming from. The plan to put a camera over his desk hadn't worked, but maybe there was another way. Grabbing his phone again, he texted Nolan:

Are you around today?

Finally pushing himself out of bed, Slater went into the kitchen. Sick of pickles and peanut butter, he sniffed at an ancient little take-out tub of salsa fresca. It seemed edible, so he downed it, then ate some olives. As he was getting dressed, Nolan's reply came:

Sunday's my day off. What's up?

Slater texted back:

Meet me in the Arts District later. I'll buy you lunch.

Before he had time to set the phone down, Nolan replied:

Deal.

Slater grinned and texted him the name of a breakfast place he knew that did some vegan stuff.

Once he was dressed, he stepped out his front door, not bothering to lock it, and knocked on Grace's.

Dressed in a blue cardigan, she pulled it open and smiled at him, the corners of her rheumy eyes creasing.

"Hi there, handsome."

"You're in a good mood," Slater said.

"It's not every day a strapping young buck knocks at my door."

Slater chuckled. "Have you got a minute?"

"Come in," she said, and stepped aside for him, waving to the sofa. "Do you want a coffee?"

"Sure," he said, and stood in the living room, watching as she filled two mugs from the tap and put them in the microwave.

Taking a jar of instant coffee out of the cupboard, she called to him, "So what's going on?"

"How would you feel about taking an acting job?" Slater said. "You'd have to fake a medical crisis."

Setting the jar on the counter, Grace stepped out of the kitchen, grimacing and grabbing at her shoulder and her neck. "I'm having chest pains," she said, her voice shrill, and then her face contorted in agony. "Did somebody burn the toast?" Grace staggered a few steps, made a gagging noise, and her eyes rolled up into her head.

Slater laughed. "Hey, one health issue at a time. Can you collapse and play disoriented?"

"What's the floor going to be like?" she said.

He thought about it for a second. "The performance venue is carpeted," he said, and eyeing Grace's, added, "It's something like yours."

Grace groaned, and wheezed, and twisted sideways, clutching her shoulder, then lurched and dropped to the carpet. "Where am I?" she said, propped on one elbow, her other hand reaching for the ceiling, blinking and gazing vacantly around the room.

"You're a natural," Slater said. "You're also a lot more agile than I expected."

"I'm old, but that doesn't mean I'm infirm," she said, frowning at him. The microwave beeped, and Grace climbed to her feet, striding into the kitchen. "At my age," she called to him, "you just hope that doesn't happen for real."

She swirled a spoonful of brown crystals into each mug and brought them out, handing one to Slater, who joined her on the sofa. Turning toward her, he told her about Abner, and outlined the plan he'd formulated, glad that she seemed to understand everything and wasn't at all dubious.

"You'll need to look stupid rich," Slater added, sipping the ersatz coffee. "Like a bored Westside hausfrau."

"Ladies who lunch," Grace said, nodding. "I know them well. I can get my hair done that way, if you're willing to fund it."

"What about clothes?"

"Clothes are easy. I'll look online at what wealthy women are wearing these days, then get knockoffs in the Fashion District. To really sell it, though, I'll need jewelry, and it has to be real."

"I know a jewelry guy," Slater said. "How much for the hair and the clothes?"

"I'm guessing two or three hundred for the salon, and maybe the same for an outfit."

"Can you make all that happen yourself? I know you don't drive anymore."

"The metro goes there. It won't be a problem."

Slater pulled out his wad of cash and gave her six C-notes.

The bills disappeared into Grace's cardigan.

"It's exciting to be on a job. When are we doing this?"

"I'm thinking tomorrow. Is that enough time?" He sipped at the tepid liquid in his mug.

Her eyebrows shot up. "I'd better get cracking, then. And I will need to get paid."

"Of course. Your stage time will be maybe half an hour, plus all the prep work. What will that cost me?"

"What's your total budget for this job?"

Slater grinned. "You're good at this. How much do you want?"

Grace frowned thoughtfully. "Your apartment must cost about the same as mine. How about a month's rent?"

Slater considered that. It was a lot of dough, but he needed her, and he knew she could pull it off.

"Deal," he said, meeting her eye, then rose and set his mug in the sink. "Call me if you need anything."

Trotting down to the garage, he had to grin. Grace was so game, and she was focused—he didn't have to tell her anything twice. He grabbed a couple of screwdrivers from the toolbox on the counter in his garage, then went back upstairs to his apartment. Sitting on the carpet in the living room, he assembled the fan, standing it on its base. When he plugged it in, it was quiet, and the breeze felt good. Maybe it would be useful. Yanking out the plug, he texted Conrad:

Thanks for the fan. It works great.

People loved that kind of thing, he'd been told—gratitude, humility, pretty words. It wouldn't hurt him once in a while to try to act like a human being.

Stuffing his phone back in his pants, he folded up the box the fan had come in and carried it down to the trash on his way out.

Sunday traffic was light, but the lot next to Andy's building was busy, the attendant happy to take his money. When Andy came to the door, he was wearing jeans and a knit sweater, his arms already looped into the cuffs of his crutches.

"Wow—you actually have pants," Slater said.

"Cut the snark," Andy said. "I'm doing you a favor today."

After he'd locked up, they walked to the elevator.

"I was actually thinking about that," Slater said. "Maybe I don't need to go with you. I'm feeling a lot better."

"You can't take it back," Andy said firmly, stepping inside when the doors slid open. "You're here. This is happening."

"I figured as much. Are we driving?"

"It's just a couple of blocks. We'll hoof it."

Walking with Andy was leisurely, but it was annoying to see how people reacted to him. Most pedestrians studiously ignored each other on busy sidewalks, but Andy got lots of looks: curiosity, sympathy, even distaste. They crossed Broadway and headed south. Slater's heart was pounding just seeing how people looked at him, and he scanned their faces, ready to punch out any potential idiot harasser. How did Andy put up with it?

"How was Albuquerque?" Andy said.

"Easy to get around. Big wide streets with nobody on them."

"What did you find out?"

"That bar is definitely Abner's," Slater said.

Andy paused in front of a building on Main Street, a new construction, and slapped the accessibility button with one of his sticks.

"Isn't this a Skid Row thing?" Slater said, looking into the lobby.

"Maybe, yeah. There's classrooms, and I know people live upstairs." Andy navigated through the door once it had swung open.

"So I've finally hit Skid Row," Slater said.

"You don't actually … sleep here, so you can't claim that." He stopped outside a door, with a sheet of printer paper taped to it that said MEETING, and turned to Slater. "You don't have to say anything. Just listen."

Slater opened the door for him to find a small room with ten or twelve people in it. The meeting hadn't started yet, and some of them were chatting or sitting quietly in the chairs, which were arranged in a circle. A couple of women stood near the door at a table with a coffee urn on it. Several voices called out Andy's name as he made his way in.

Two or three of the men and one of the women looked like they were on the skids, Slater thought, assessing the crowd. Others were dressed like they had means. If this was their nearest meeting, they were likely residents of the pricey neighborhoods abutting Skid Row. Most of them were in their twenties and thirties, although a couple of the rough characters looked older.

Andy sat beside a dark-complected woman wearing a red top and a push-up bra.

"Who's the pigeon?" she asked, eyeing Slater as he sat on Andy's other side.

"He's not a pigeon. He's a friend of mine," Andy said. "Kate, this is Slater."

Slater nodded in acknowledgment, then quietly asked him, "What's a pigeon? Where I come from, that means a sucker."

"It's kind of the same thing. It means a new recruit."

"I'm not a pigeon."

"What did I just … tell her?" Andy demanded.

A guy holding a binder called order, and the few people still standing took seats. He talked about some procedural matters at first. Slater sat with his arms folded.

"It's nice to see some new faces here," the leader said finally, eyeing Slater.

Slater narrowed his eyes, a subtle challenge, but the guy was only acknowledging his presence, and called on the woman beside Andy. She told a story about being tempted to use again, how easy it was to get drugs, even when you weren't looking, and how hard it was to be sober. It was easy to see why, Slater thought—she was soft, easily influenced, had no self-control. But nobody told her anything like that, which struck him as a missed opportunity.

Next a guy across the circle gave his own spiel. He spoke about how staying clean gave him clarity. He could see his life more objectively, he said, and make better decisions. That made some sense, although the guy still looked like a junky—skinny, rough skin, hollowed-out cheeks, and that terrible haircut, buzzed on the sides and drooping into his eyes.

After the meeting wound up, people stood around talking. Leaning on his crutches, Andy gabbed with his friends, his tone animated. Slater had no intention of making small talk with strangers or answering any stupid questions, so he went to the table with the coffee and the doughnuts and filled a paper cup, sipping it and standing near the door.

Eventually Andy glanced at him, then pulled himself away from his conversation, and they walked out together.

Once they were outside on the street, Andy said, "Want to grab a coffee at the diner?"

Slater checked the time. "Sure," he said, and dropped his paper cup into a trash can.

The diner was just a few doors down, but they were walking at a sedate pace, and a guy with greasy slicked-back hair, his hands jammed in the pockets of his green camo jacket, caught up to them and walked abreast, eyeing Slater. He said something in Spanish.

"*No comprendo,*" Slater said.

"*Zoquete,*" the guy insisted.

"I only have the one language, bub," Slater said. "Spread out."

"Antifreeze, dummy," he said. "I just saw you come out of that meeting."

Slater stopped, and raised his voice. "What the fuck are you talking about?"

"Smack. I can set you up."

"You're selling outside a twelve-step meeting?" Andy said. "That's … low, man. Shame on you."

"It's called targeted marketing," he said, "and

I'm not talking to the spaz."

Still looking at Andy, the guy didn't see it coming when Slater punched him on the jaw. It wasn't a knockout blow, but it got his attention, spinning his head, and he stumbled back.

"Hey—no violence," the guy shouted.

"Stop it," Andy demanded.

"Call a cop," Slater said, stepping toward the guy. "Go ahead—do it." Lunging at him, he landed one more blow, on the guy's shoulder blade as he twisted to get away.

Trotting up the sidewalk, he turned back. "Fuck you," he shouted. "Junky fucking psycho."

Slater waved languorously. "Keep moving."

"Why did you do that?" Andy demanded, scowling in anger.

"He's a dick," Slater said, watching to make sure the guy wasn't coming back, then turning to face him.

"What if he'd been carrying a gun, or a blade?"

"I would have taken it away from him."

Andy scoffed and started walking, working his crutches. "Such a hard-ass. I don't need defending."

"That's not what it was about," Slater said. "He was being a dick."

"That's true," Andy admitted, and heaved open the door to the diner.

Eyeing his crutches, the host seated them at a

table near the front door.

"Just coffee, and bring me a straw," Andy told the waitress. He waited while she poured steaming java into their mugs, then said to Slater, "That wasn't so difficult, was it?"

"Sitting there wasn't. Listening to the stories was a bit tedious."

"None of it resonated with you?"

Slater thought about it. "Maybe the thing about clarity. I can see how that might kick in if you're sober for a while."

"Being sober is the long game. First you have to get clean, or in your case, dry out."

"Is that the first step?" Slater said, sipping at his mug.

"The first step is admitting you're powerless over your addiction."

"That doesn't really click. I'm not powerless. I can do whatever I want."

"The fact that you wanted to go to a meeting means you know you're powerless," Andy said. "Just showing up today was huge. It means things are out of hand, and you know it's OK to ask for help."

The waitress handed Andy a straw, and he jabbed it into his coffee mug.

Slater watched for a moment as he sipped. "I just don't know if meetings are for me. I'd rather sort it out myself."

"With your booze rules? That doesn't really seem to be working."

"I have control over it," Slater said firmly.

"With alcoholics it's always the ego," Andy said, frowning. "But then there's the secrets, and the guilt, and the shame."

"Fuck you," Slater snapped.

Andy leaned toward him, his gaze intent despite his undulating posture. "I'm not judging you. It's not personal. Just think about it—do you really have control?"

Slater bit his lip and looked into his mug, swirling its contents.

"I know you, Slater," Andy said intently. "I know you get it."

Slater folded his arms, and they sat in silence for a while.

"I should go," he said finally. "I have stuff to do today."

"People to slap around?"

"Only if they deserve it."

Andy scoffed and reached for his sticks. "You're paying."

Slater went to the register, and by the time he'd settled up, Andy was on his way out the door.

Walking back toward Broadway, Slater said, "Have you told your story at one of those meetings?"

"Many times," Andy said. "It's called a share."

"I'm glad you have peers that you can connect with."

"That's the whole idea. It's worked for a lot of people for a long time."

"Thanks for taking me," Slater said, pausing in front of the entrance to Andy's building.

"Sure," Andy said simply.

Slater leaned in to kiss him good-bye, and lingered in it, resting his hand on the back of Andy's neck. The guy was such a good kisser.

From nearby he heard someone call, "Get a room."

Slater snapped upright, fists balled, ready to fight. It was the woman in the red shirt from the meeting, smiling at them as she passed, heading up the street.

Andy tapped Slater's calf with his stick. "Settle down. It's Kate—she's just joking."

He chuckled and met his eye. "I knew that."

"You could have fooled me."

Walking around to his car, Slater felt lighter. He wasn't planning on ever going to another meeting, but at least he knew now what they were like.

____

The Arts District was busy on Sunday, and it took a few minutes to find a meter near the restaurant. Walking up on the place, there was a small crowd waiting outside for tables, Nolan among them, wearing a bright plaid shirt and form-fitting tan chinos. He flashed a smile when he saw Slater.

"I put my name in already," he said, stepping over to the edge of the sidewalk.

"Smart," Slater said. "No paint store today?"

"It's a place for contractors and professional painters, and they don't work on Sunday. What's your favorite paint color?"

Slater's eyes narrowed. "You sound like a shrink."

"Why would a shrink ask you something like that?"

"To get insights into your crazy, I suppose. What's your favorite paint color?"

"It depends on the room size," Nolan said, gesturing with both hands. "Big rooms can go dark red, or navy blue, or warm green. Small rooms need a light touch—saturated yellow, maybe, or eggshell."

"I should have you do my office."

Holding Slater's gaze, he spoke earnestly, his expression deadpan. "If it's anything like your apartment, I'd recommend euthanasia."

Slater had to laugh.

A harried-looking woman stepped outside, menus in hand. "Mr. Nolan?" she called.

Stepping toward her, he said, "It's just Nolan."

Slater followed them inside. The place was crowded and loud, and once they were sitting and perusing the menu, Nolan leaned forward and said, "What's good that's vegan?"

"You're not vegan," Slater said, looking up at him.

"No, but I'm not going to sit here and eat nasty *carnitas* in your face."

"It doesn't bother me," he said, but when the waiter came around, he ordered the same thing Slater was having, a veganized Florentine with cornbread on the side.

After they'd eaten, stuffing bills into the

folder with the check, Slater said, "I want to look at shoes. Any interest?"

"I actually need a pair of dress shoes," he said. "Is it that kind of store?"

"It's exactly that kind of store. Dress shoes with no leather in them, and it's within walking distance."

"Vegan shoes," Nolan said, following him out to the street. "That's such a cool synchronicity."

The suggestion that anything supernatural was involved made Slater bristle, but he wasn't about to reveal that he'd watched Nolan perusing shoes online when he was sitting at his desk in Abner's office.

The sidewalks were crowded as they walked, people eating out and plying the neighborhood's trendy galleries and pubs.

"Why do you need dress shoes?" Nolan said, linking his arm through Slater's. "Does the fiber company send you out on sales calls?"

"Fiber's just one of the things I do."

"It sucks that you have to have more than one job at your age. What else do you do?"

"I'm in insurance."

Slater stopped in front of the shoe store, a chic conversion of an old industrial space, in its former life a single-story warehouse or maybe a body shop. Today the brick had been sandblasted, glass lined the erstwhile loading bay, and planter boxes of horsetail flanked the entrance. Designers liked that stuff because it looked like bamboo, but it had become so ubiquitous that it was starting to look dated. Hopefully the trend would ebb—it was hard to take care of, and piggy with the water. There were much better dryland plants that would look way more dramatic.

As they stepped inside, the clerk, a spiffy guy with a plaid jacket and little round glasses, his hair in a high top, subtly looked them over. Slater ignored him, and Nolan wandered around, picking up samples.

Turning to Slater, he held up a black brogue. "These would be perfect, if they were about a third the price."

"What size are you?" Slater asked.

"Ten."

Slater called to the clerk, "Show me those in a ten."

"Coming up," he said cheerfully, and stepped through the doorway into the stock room.

"There's no point," Nolan said. "I can't afford them."

"Just try them on."

The clerk returned with a box, setting it next to a little bench. Nolan sat and untied his sneakers, pulling them off. After he'd knotted the brogues, he rose and walked around the store.

"They look fabulous on you," the clerk said.

"They fit really well," Nolan said, walking back.

"I'm going to buy them for you," Slater said.

Nolan frowned. "Why would you do that?"

"Because I'm going to ask for your help with something later."

"With what?"

"I can't tell you that now."

"I don't need a sugar daddy," Nolan said.

"That's not what I'm doing," Slater snapped.

The clerk put his hand on Nolan's arm. "If the gentleman wants to buy you a pair of shoes, you should let him. If you change your mind later, you can bring them back."

"I'm not a gentleman," Slater said, scowling at him.

"And I'm not a whore," Nolan said, raising his voice.

"These are imported from England," the clerk said gravely. "They're totally worth it."

Slater sighed in frustration. "This has no connection to sex. I want to hire you to do a job. I should have explained that before. I'm doing this wrong."

"Hire me, and pay me in shoes? Is it legit work?"

"No, but it's not sex either."

Nolan chuckled, his angry pride melting. "Fine—buy me the damn shoes."

The clerk beamed and scooped up the box.

"Will you be wearing them out today?"

"I'll stick with my sneakers," Nolan said, and sat to take off the brogues.

At the register, Slater dug in his pocket, but he didn't have enough cash—funding Grace had depleted his bankroll. Here he was, acting like a bigshot, and he couldn't even pay for the freaking shoes. How stupid was that?

"Damn it," he muttered, digging deeper and finding only fins and singles.

"Problem?" the clerk asked.

"I'll have to use plastic," he said, and passed him a card. He hated doing that because it created a data trail, fixing his whereabouts to a time and place, for anyone to look up later. He hated feeling limited like that, having to remember what he could and couldn't reasonably deny.

The clerk ran the card, and smiling at Nolan, handed him a bag with the shoebox in it.

Once they were out on the sidewalk, Nolan said, "Did anyone ever tell you that you're kind of weird?"

"My whole life, toots," Slater said flatly.

"Tell me what you want to hire me for."

"I'll get to that, but first, do you want to hook up? Watching you get steamed back there was kind of a turn-on."

Nolan laughed. "I thought these were no-strings shoes."

"You don't have to sleep with me because I bought you those."

"I get it, Slater. You already explained that—sort of. I want to sleep with you. But we'll have to go to your place."

Climbing into the Thunderbird, Nolan reached over and put a hand on his face. Slater tensed up, but Nolan just wanted to kiss him, and he leaned into it. Behind them a car beeped, waiting for the space. Slater pulled away from Nolan and glanced in the rearview, then started the engine and nosed into the street.

"So why don't you have a husband, or a fiancé, or a boyfriend?" Nolan said.

"I tried that. It didn't work out. Why don't you?"

"I'm sure I will eventually. There is a guy I'm interested in."

"What's he like?"

"He lives in my neighborhood. Everyone calls him Chino. I see him on the train."

"Does he know you exist?" Slater said, checking the cross traffic and turning onto Fifth Street.

"We say hello."

"So ask him out."

"Yeah, it's not that easy."

"Do you want me to look into him for you? I can find out if he's bad news."

Nolan watched him for a moment. "Is that a

service offered by the fiber company, or the insurance company?"

Slater focused on the road, and soon turned into his alley, pausing while the garage door rolled up. Once they were upstairs, Nolan dropped the bag with his shoes beside the sofa, and by the time Slater had the door bolted, he had his shirt off.

"I can't keep my eyes off you," Nolan said. "Why is that?"

Slater stepped toward him and pulled him close, running his hands over the warm skin of his back, his smooth shoulder blades.

"This time, do you want to fuck me?" Nolan said.

Slater led him into the bedroom, and Nolan grabbed Slater's belt, unbuckling it and popping open the buttons on his jeans. Slater put his hands on Nolan's waist, sliding his fingers into his chinos and pushing them off, and soon they were both naked. Pulling him onto the bed, Nolan grabbed Slater's cock, squeezing it and humming. Under his breath he said, "Oh, yeah."

Slater grabbed a condom from the bedside drawer and rolled it on, then kissed Nolan's neck as he worked his lubed fingers inside him, eliciting a gasp. Pulling up his knees, Slater penetrated him, moving slowly at first. Nolan's eyes were closed, but he had his hands on Slater's thighs, guiding him closer. Slater built up speed until he was pounding him, and as he was getting close, Nolan cried out and came. Feeling that was a turn-on, and Slater came too, thrusting deeper. Finally he pulled away.

Stretching out on the bed, he tossed the condom onto the floor and got close to Nolan.

"I did it again," Nolan said, running his hand over Slater's chest. "I came too fast. That was just so hot, I couldn't help it."

"It's good that it works that way for you. You're lucky."

Nolan laughed, flashing those perfect teeth.

"All right—truth time," Slater said.

Nolan scooted up the bed and shoved a pillow behind his back. "The facts," he said, and clapped his hands, frowning in mock seriousness.

Slater turned to face him, propping his head on his arm. "I need you to help me get into Abner's office."

His eyes grew wide. "That's what the shoes were for?"

"Forget about the shoes. That's over with."

"Why do you want to get in there?"

"I need to look at his files. Just for a few minutes."

"You're doing that for your insurance company?"

"In a way," Slater lied. "I'm trying to find out what he's doing for his clients that's not on the level."

"It's moot anyway. I don't have a key to that office."

"That's why we'll do it when he's there."

"How?"

"I'll lay out the details later."

Nolan frowned and bit his lip. Finally he said, "It's so unethical."

"That's why I'll pay you."

"More than the shoes?"

"Forget the shoes," Slater said. "Think cash payment for work performed."

Nolan watched him for a moment. "How much will you pay me?"

Slater had to concentrate not to smile. It was a done deal now—all that remained was setting the price. Paying him was a necessary part of it, because it meant he was complicit, and couldn't rat him out later, or claim Slater had tricked him into helping.

"How much do you want?" Slater asked.

"What will I have to do?"

"First you have to unlock the door from Abner's office into the hall. Then, after you serve the coffee to the client, you have to leave the office for a while. Go downstairs and get a snack."

"That's it?"

"Simple, right?"

"My breaks are fifteen minutes."

"That works," Slater said. "You disappear for

that long. What about unlocking the door?"

Nolan frowned in thought. "Abner does go out between appointments. I think he goes to the vending machines in the lobby. His office door closes on a spring but he doesn't lock it, so I could get in there."

"When he comes to work, does he go through your office, or his private door to the hall?"

"My office, always. He wants me to know that he's in."

"Perfect," Slater said. "So you know what you have to do. What's that worth?"

Nolan sighed, looking away. Finally he said, "Five hundred bucks."

Slater had planned to be outraged if he wanted more than two grand, and would have tried to talk him down if he wanted more than one.

"That's a lot of dough," he said, running his hand along Nolan's thigh. "Tell you what—I can swing it."

"Half up front," Nolan said, meeting his gaze.

"You drive a hard bargain, son."

"When are you going to do this?"

"You're working there tomorrow, right?"

"OK, wow. That's really soon."

"It is," Slater said, "but you don't have much to prepare."

"I know there are clients scheduled."

"Just play it cool," Slater said. "It'll be fine."

Nolan nodded, and shifted closer, and ran his fingers through Slater's hair. His eyes went soft, his gaze intent.

"Don't look at me like that," Slater said, closing his eyes, enjoying the feeling of Nolan's fingers on his scalp.

"Like what?"

Like you're beautiful, and vulnerable, and available, Slater thought. But he didn't say that.

Pulling away, breaking the spell, Slater went into the bathroom and closed the door, turning on the tap in the sink and then sitting in front of it, opening the cabinet and reaching up inside for his cash bundle. Counting out a grand, he sealed the bag again and stuffed it back in its place.

In the bedroom, Nolan was getting dressed. Slater grabbed his jeans from the floor and stuffed the cash in the pocket, peeling off three hundreds and handing them over.

"Thanks," Nolan said, happy to see them.

"Can I drive you home?"

"You have a metro station right up the block. Why do car people never even notice those?"

Slater chuckled. "I have some work to do, but if I can make this happen tomorrow, can we go through the plan tonight?"

"Sure," Nolan said, buttoning his shirt, but concern clouded his face.

"It's going to be fine. Think of it as an adventure."

Nolan nodded and went to the front door, picking up the bag with his new shoes.

"Later, hot stuff," he said, and let himself out.

Once he was gone, Slater pulled his satchel out from behind the sofa and extracted his laptop, then sat on the recliner. Logging into Abner's calendar software using the credentials he'd gleaned from the other receptionist, he looked at the schedule for tomorrow. Abner had two blocks filled in, one in the morning and one at three. Grace would fit nicely at 1:30, he decided, and typed in "Grace Higgins." That wasn't her surname, but it would be simpler to use her real first name.

Folding the computer closed and stowing it again, he got dressed and locked up, then knocked on Grace's door.

Pulling it open, she glanced past him into the hall and said quietly, "What's the plan?"

"We're on for tomorrow. The meeting is at 1:30. I'll pick you up."

"I'm glad it's a bit later," she said. "I wasn't sure when you'd need me, so I got a hair appointment at nine."

Slater nodded. "I'll stop by later with the jewelry and we'll do a run-through."

TWELVE

On the way down the stairs to his car, Slater steeled himself for the task ahead. A while back he'd hooked up with a jeweler named Vahan. The guy was kind of raunchy, but he'd been into Slater. He knew where Vahan's shop was, and he knew that he had a wife. Slater wasn't about to blackmail the guy with that, as he had no idea how unsavory Vahan really was, or how dialed in to the underworld he might be. But he could use it to apply a little pressure if he needed to.

The Jewelry District was downtown, halfway to Slater's office, and he parked at a meter, double-checking the signs to make sure it was free on Sunday. The shop was huge, shared by several jewelers, with rows of brightly lit glass-topped counters filled with shiny baubles. A couple of the vendors were talking to customers, and Vahan was here, behind the counter at the far end, for the moment on his own. Of course he was here—he had the immigrant work ethic, putting in long hours.

Vahan had a beautiful Roman nose and dark coloring, maybe Armenian. The guy had put on weight, he saw, and what was with that awful haircut, neglected and half covering his ears? It was effortlessly easy to get a decent cut in this town.

Looking up, Vahan smiled in recognition as Slater approached, his gums showing above his teeth.

"Sweet Slater," he said. "How are you?"

"I don't need a haircut, but you do. Doesn't your wife remind you to go to the barber?"

Vahan laughed. "You're such a prick. Can't I just admire your lovely face without you talking about her?"

"Don't call me lovely," Slater said, resting his hands on his hips. "Listen, I need to borrow a couple of pieces of your inventory. Just for a day or two. I have to make an elderly woman look rich."

"I don't rent out jewelry," he said flatly.

"I thought you might make an exception for an old friend."

Vahan sighed. "Come in the back. I might have something for you." Looking past Slater into the shop, he called to a woman who wasn't talking to a customer, standing behind a counter with her hands folded behind her. She nodded and said something back to him. Slater wasn't even sure what language they were speaking.

As he opened the low gate at the side of his counter, Vahan gestured for him to follow, leading him back into a tiny office with grimy linoleum, a cluttered desk, and battered old file cabinets. Closing the door, Vahan twisted the deadbolt.

"You know what I want from you," he said, eyeing Slater.

Slater dropped his chin, holding his gaze, and said softly, "Vahan, you make me feel like a whore."

Vahan giggled, his eyes bright. "On your knees, whore."

Slater stepped closer, and Vahan put his hands on his shoulders, pushing him down.

"Please don't make me," Slater said, a feigned and half-hearted plea, and sank to his knees.

"Suck my dick, you piece of trash."

Slater unzipped the fly of Vahan's ill-fitting polyester pants. The guy already had a chubby, and he took it into his mouth, bracing himself with one hand and closing his eyes so that he wouldn't get nauseous. Vahan was sweaty and ripe and didn't trim his body hair. He never should have hooked up with him the first time.

"Yeah," Vahan grunted. "Fuck, yeah. You filthy whore."

It struck Slater then—in no way was he enjoying this, and he was doing it to get jewelry. He really was a whore.

Finally Vahan came, straining and grunting, and Slater looked up at him, making the best puppy-dog eyes he could muster.

Grinning, Vahan mussed his hair, seemingly satisfied. "I wish you'd come around and do that every afternoon."

"You'd have to buy me kneepads," Slater said, getting to his feet.

Vahan guffawed, showing his gummy smile. "I have a couple of pieces that might work for your lady."

Checking his fly, he unlocked the door and led Slater out to the shop floor. Slater stepped through the gate and stood across the counter from him. Vahan slid open a display case and lifted out a tray, setting it on top.

"Sparkly," Slater said, assessing the jewelry it contained.

Vahan picked up a pair of earrings and a bracelet. "These are a set."

"They're diamonds?"

"Of course they're diamonds, you philistine."

"I can't really tell," Slater said, feeling the heft of the bracelet. What mattered was whether

Abner could tell. Grace would know for sure whether this stuff would pass.

"Do you want a necklace too?" Vahan said.

"I'm not sure. It's for a daytime meeting at an office."

"So no necklace," Vahan said, and reached into the case, pulling out a pin in the shape of a swan, bejeweled in dark blue stones and more diamonds. "How does this look?" He set it beside the other pieces.

"You're the pro. If you think it's what I need, I'll take it."

Vahan grabbed a clipboard and spent a minute hunched over the counter, writing in the lines of an invoice. Straightening up and twisting the sheet toward Slater, he said, "Contact info, and sign at the bottom."

Slater filled in the boxes with his office address, surprised at the total Vahan had written at the bottom, $38,500. It didn't look like that much bling.

"Now I know where to find you if you don't bring them back," Vahan said, scanning the page.

"You'll have it all back on Tuesday. So how much to rent this stuff?"

Vahan grinned. "You already paid."

After he packed the pieces in little dark-blue jewelry boxes, he put them in a black paper bag and handed it to Slater.

"Thank you for your custom," Vahan said, with a louche wink.

Walking out, he wondered how much he could pad his bill to Marisol to cover sexual degradation. He needed a drink, he realized, stepping outside into the twilight, and headed down to Seventh Street. Around the corner, on the second floor over a burger joint, was a dark little pub that he knew. It wasn't busy this early, he saw, climbing the stairs, and he sat at the bar.

"A tequila shot and an order of fries," he told the bartender, setting the black bag of jewelry on the bar top, then digging a C-note out of his pocket and dropping it in front of him.

When the shot came up, he slammed it, feeling the warmth in his belly. It fit his booze rules because it was after dark, and even though he still had work to do, it was just the one. As he waited for the fries, he pulled out his phone and texted Nolan:

Meet me at my office tonight?

He added the street address. Nolan's reply came just as his food did:

I'll be there in an hour.

Slater felt a little buzzed, but greasy food would soak up the tequila. He ate with his fingers, then scooped up his change and the jewelry and walked back to his car.

The parking lot at his office was empty, and he opened the Thunderbird's trunk to get a roll of duct tape. He took Vahan's jewelry with him too—no way was he going to leave it unattended, and be on the hook for forty grand.

The building was dead quiet, making the hum and rattle of the elevator machinery seem loud. Stepping into his office, he flicked on the lights and bolted the door.

In the safe he counted out the cash he'd need to pay Grace, then noted it on the envelope, stuffing the bills in his pocket and locking it again. Settling into his chair, he swung his feet up on his desk, not touching his computer but rather gazing at the faded painting of the artichokes. Why had that image appealed to him? It was just a bowl of vegetables, and the colors were washed out, probably from sitting in the sun, like Ken in Albuquerque, and that manager at the Live Wire.

In his mind he went through what was going to happen tomorrow, trying to anticipate what might go wrong, planning for those contingencies. A knock at the door jolted him from his thoughts, and he rose to pull it open.

Nolan had on the same tan chinos, pleasingly accentuating his shape, but he'd changed his shirt and wore a dark bomber jacket, hands jammed in the pockets.

"You're really here," Nolan said, relief in his tone. "I thought I had the wrong building. This place is all clothing factories, and everything's closed."

"It's not all factories. There are a couple offices like this."

Nolan nodded to the lettering on the door. "It says 'investigations.' I thought you worked for an insurance company. Who's Maximilian?"

"My business partner," Slater said. "Are you going to come in?"

He stepped inside. "What's really going on, man?"

"Nothing nefarious," Slater said, locking the deadbolt. "I work contracts. Most of them are for an insurance company."

Nolan sighed, and pulled off his jacket, absently hanging it on the coatrack. That was a first, Slater thought—no one ever used it. The woman who'd rented them the office furniture had thrown it in to make the place look more finished.

"So you're an investigator, and you're investigating Abner," he said. "Is it really for his insurance?"

Slater held his gaze. "You know Abner is shady. You told me that yourself."

"Right."

"That's what I'm investigating."

Nolan took a deep breath and nodded. "Why didn't you buy any shoes today for yourself?"

"I didn't see any that I liked."

"Do you really work for the fiber company?"

"That was just a way for me to case your office."

"The facts," Nolan said, his brow furrowing, watching Slater. "I guess it all fits. You lied to me, though."

"Can you understand why?"

"I get it. You didn't know how tight I was with Abner." He glanced around the little office. "Is this desk for your receptionist?"

"Interesting question. It's more about not wanting an empty front office. Even if we could afford it, we don't really need a receptionist."

"Do you even have a coffeemaker?"

"There's nothing like that." Slater gestured at the Spartan space. "We get takeout. The men's room down the hall has a sink if you need water."

Nolan chuckled. "I don't want coffee. I'm just curious."

"Come in, then," Slater said, and went into his office.

"You're allowed to paint in here, you know," Nolan said, following him.

"What's wrong with white?"

"Commercial landlords do that to show the space, but tenants paint when they come in. It's that industrial matte white, so you don't even have to prime it."

Slater grinned and dropped into his desk chair. "What color would you put in here?"

"The outer office I'd do really soft orange, almost pastel, to put your clients at ease, but warm enough to show them that you're on the ball. In here, maybe periwinkle."

"Periwinkle is a color?" Slater said. "I know it as an invasive weed. People used to plant it as ground cover. We'd rip it out whenever we found it."

"You're a gardener too?"

"I studied horticulture in college."

"Periwinkle is kind of a bright purple-blue."

"Like the flower, maybe," Slater said.

Nolan looked around. "Why don't you have a window in here?"

"It's on the other side, in Max's office."

Stepping out, Nolan went to look. "I'd have to meet the guy, but I'm thinking lime green."

"I bet he'd love that."

Nolan came back and sat in the chair in front of Slater's desk, folding his arms. "So what do I have to do tomorrow? I need details."

Slater leaned back, lacing his fingers behind his head. "My operative is on Abner's calendar for 1:30. Make sure Abner keeps the meeting. If he questions it, tell him the woman is rich and she needs to stash some cash, maybe overseas."

"I wouldn't normally know things like that."

"Tell him anyway, if he asks," Slater said. "If he's suspicious, tell him you took her call on Friday."

Nolan nodded. "That could have happened."

"Sometime before the meeting, you have to unlock the door to the hall."

"That's easy, right? I just flip the knob."

"The handle is probably set to lock itself when it closes, even if the deadbolt is unlocked. You might be able to disengage it, but that might require a key."

"I don't have keys for that door."

"So you'll have to tape it open." Slater reached for the roll of duct tape on his desk and handed it to him.

"This is getting complicated. Why don't I just go through his files for you? I'm there anyway."

"You don't know what to look for. It has to be me."

Nolan sighed and looked at the roll of tape.

"Let me show you," Slater said, and got up, then crouched in front of the door to his office. "It'll be on a spring, like this." He pressed in the latch to demonstrate, then took the roll of tape and tore off a strip with a loud squawk. "The tape is too wide, and you don't want it to show, so you rip it in half." Pressing the narrow strip over the latch, Slater rubbed it with the heel of his hand to make it adhere. Rising, he pushed the door closed, then pulled it open. "Now I can just walk in."

"How will you know when to do that?" Nolan said.

"After you serve the coffee, you call me on your cell, and put it on speaker, and leave it on your desk. That way I can hear what's happening in your office. And when you come out into the hall, give me the high sign."

"I can do that."

"If things aren't going to plan, you can give me a thumbs-down, and I won't go in." Slater peeled the tape off the door, then handed the roll to Nolan. "You try."

Nolan deftly pulled off a strip and tore it in half, then pressed it over the latch.

"Good," Slater said, "but pull the tape taut as you stick it on. That way it'll stay tight."

He made him do it again, and then again.

"Dude, I get it," Nolan said finally.

"If you practice now, you won't be nervous doing it tomorrow."

"I'm not so sure about that," he said. "So why do I have to be gone when your friend is there?"

"She's going to have a medical emergency, and then lead Abner into the front office. If you're there, he can just dump her on you. So you need to be out."

"And his office door closes itself," Nolan said, grinning at him, "so he won't see you go in the back. How did you think of that?"

"My job is basically about dealing with low-lifes, so outsmarting a crook is part of the deal."

"I guess I never really thought of Abner as a crook." His expression shifted. "Do you think it's going to get violent?"

"It's just an old woman having a heart attack," Slater said, gesturing casually. "I won't even see Abner, and I'll only be in there a few minutes."

"OK." Nolan nodded.

"Now tell me again," Slater said, "exactly what you're going to do."

With a sigh he dropped into the chair, but he talked his way through it. All the details were clear, and eventually Slater was satisfied that he had it right.

"One other thing," Slater said. "The security camera in your office—do you know where it records to?"

"It's wireless, so probably to the cloud, right? I don't have access to that. I do know it's plugged into the power strip under my desk. The cord is inside the wall, but it comes out again at the bottom. The camera was offline for a few days once because it had come unplugged. Abner was pissed."

"So you can disable it."

"You want me to unplug it tomorrow?" Nolan said.

"That might seem hinky. Let's not."

Rising, he handed Nolan the roll of duct tape, and Nolan tucked it into his backpack.

"Can I drive you home?" Slater asked.

"That would be great."

Slater grabbed the black paper bag with the jewelry, and on the way out, said, "Don't forget your jacket."

"I would have," Nolan said, plucking it off the rack, and flashed him that beautiful smile.

Climbing into the Thunderbird, Nolan rolled down the window despite the cold evening. Following his directions, Slater navigated onto Alameda and south to Huntington Park, turning on a street with tightly spaced bungalows, iron fences out front, bars on every window.

"You live here on your own?" Slater asked, pulling into the end of the driveway and eyeing the house.

"With my parents."

"You're going to do fine tomorrow."

"I'm not worried," Nolan said, leaning over to kiss him good-bye. Pulling away, he studied Slater's face, then leaned in again, meeting his mouth more intently. Eventually he sat back. "Why did you say you were single?"

"No way, brother," Slater said, breathing hard.

"You need to go after that Chino. I'm a wrong guy."

Nolan pushed his hand through Slater's hair, his brow furrowing. "You're probably right." He popped open the door, but then turned back. "Did I thank you for the shoes?"

"I think so."

"Well, thanks again."

Slater watched him walk toward the house, admiring the fit of his pants. No way could he even consider spending more time with him. Slater would just screw it up, screw him up, leaving a smoking ruin of damage and destruction. Chaos. He'd ruin the kid's life.

THIRTEEN

Back in Westlake, he pulled into his garage and went up the stairs, knocking on Grace's door.

"Delivery," he announced, handing her the black paper bag from Vahan.

"Come in," she said. "Let's have a look."

Perched on the sofa with the little blue boxes between them, Grace opened each one and took out the jewelry.

"Such lovely things," she said. "I'm going to look amazing."

Slater watched her trying them on, admiring the sparkle. "Just make sure everything is on tight when you hit the carpet. That stuff is real, and I'm on the hook for it."

"Of course, dear," she said, and shot him a

quizzical smile.

Mentally Slater kicked himself. How could he mistrust Grace? She had been swimming in the cynical grimy depths since before he was born. The moment they'd met, she knew exactly who he was, understood him, saw right through him—she'd been doing work like his half a lifetime ago, and she never questioned his behavior. He was such a prick sometimes. This woman would help him steal from a toddler if he asked, slap a cop for him, lie to a judge.

Grace closed the boxes and set them back in the bag. "What exactly is the timeline?"

"Abner thinks you're coming in for advice on hiding some assets overseas. The receptionist is working with me. He's going to bring coffee into your meeting. Give him a minute to amscray after he steps out, and then you can have your medical crisis."

"And get Abner into the front office," she said.

"Don't break character in there," Slater said. "It's the only place with a security camera."

Grace raised her eyebrows. "In the 1970s, I once hustled my way onto an airliner and flew across the country without a ticket. No one ever made me. I won't break character until I'm back in this apartment."

Slater nodded. "It's not that I'm doubting your skills. I just want things to go smoothly."

"So what kind of man is he?"

"Abner? He acts cocky, but you'll see through it. He's really kind of soft and floppy."

"Easily excited?"

"I'd say so, yeah."

She nodded confidently. "It's easy to work with that type."

"I'll need a few minutes in his office," Slater said, and they talked through it, making sure she was clear on the plan.

Eventually Slater rose. "I have your fee," he said, digging in his pocket and handing her the wad of bills.

Grace folded them in half and tucked them away, not counting them. "You're pretty cavalier, paying me before I've done any work."

"I trust you as much as anyone on the planet," he said.

Grace beamed. "That's very sweet of you."

Stepping into his own apartment, he locked the door and kicked off his boots, then poured a calculated inch of bourbon into a tumbler and dropped in an ice cube. After he killed the lights, he stretched out on the sofa, and briefly considered opening his hookup app. But he was tired, and he'd been with Nolan today. He could take a night off.

Sipping the bourbon, he set the tumbler on the carpet. He hated rationing it this way. But he certainly wasn't ready for meetings full of alcoholics, sitting around whining about his problems. In his teens he'd been press-ganged into that by Doris and all those shrinks. Twelve-step wasn't for him anyway. He wasn't desperate, like those junkies at Andy's meeting. So what if he messed up and overdid it? Everyone screwed up sometimes. He just needed to take charge of things, play it cool, not let it get out of hand.

Sleep was looming, he could feel it. Taking another slurp, he put his arm over his eyes. It was all about self-control. Of course he could do that.

———◆———

For a few moments when he woke up, his mind was blissfully empty. He stared at the closet door, half open, his shirts hanging inside. Neatly pressed and ready to go. Then the day's plans crashed into his mind, and he remembered what he had to do.

Rolling out of bed, he washed up and then looked in the fridge. No peanut butter, not today. He really should go to a market. There was nothing else to eat, so he got dressed and went down to the garage. His gardening tools hung on the wall, in plain view for anyone who might break in, but in front of the Thunderbird's nose was a cabinet where he kept more sensitive stuff, mostly surveillance equipment from Svetlana. It looked like a storage cupboard, but it was heavily reinforced, and had a complex lock, more like a safe. Anyone who wanted to steal it would need a jackhammer and a few free hours.

Once he'd opened the cabinet, on one of the shelves he found the little zip-top sandwich bag, with a yellow sticky note inside it, inscribed in block letters REMOTE. Inside the bag, smaller than his thumbnail, was a tiny USB drive. Slater pulled it out and stuffed it into his pocket.

The device was new, and he'd never tried it himself, but Svetlana promised it would give him remote access to any computer it was plugged into, as long as it was powered up and online, which most computers were most of the time. It had better work—he'd gone through a lot of rig-marole in planning this incursion, plus that nasty blow job for raunchy unwashed Vahan.

Once he'd locked the cupboard, he went through the door into the hallway and out the front of the building, past the cell phone store. At the end of the block he looked around for food, and sure enough, another block away, he spotted a taco cart. Slater bought two of them, beans and rice and avocado, wrapped in foil, and ate them on the way back to his building.

Upstairs again he knocked on Grace's door. When she opened it for him, he found her trans-formed. She wore a black jacket over a print blouse, but most dramatic was her hair, styled into a swooping gray mane that curled behind her ears. Vahan's jewelry was subtle but flashy, and unmistakably expensive.

"Amazing," Slater said. "You look like a politician."

"I was aiming for East Coast heiress," Grace said, "but I'll take it."

She was speaking more slowly, so her dialect had disappeared, and her voice was louder, more confident.

"Damn, you're good," he said, taking it all in.

"Shall we? Time is money, *mon cher.*" She stepped out and locked her door. Even the way she moved felt different, more deliberate.

They rode the rickety elevator to the ground floor. Slater never used it because it was so slow, but it gave him time now to assess her look.

"No pocketbook?" he asked.

"Why would I need one?" she said, using the formal voice and waving a hand. "I left it in the car with my driver."

"Smart," Slater said, and chuckled, following her off the elevator and into his garage, where he opened the passenger door for her.

Nearing the Durham Building, he pulled over at a red curb.

"Take your time going up," he told her as she climbed out. "I have to find parking."

She waved and walked toward the entrance, and Slater pulled into traffic, circling the block and looking for a meter. Increasingly worried that he'd be late, he considered parking under the building, even though that felt like a trap. But then he saw a vehicle pull out farther along Wilshire, and raced ahead to grab the space.

Climbing out of the car, his phone rang—Nolan. Slater jammed in his earpiece and picked up the call, sliding his phone back in his pocket.

"Hey," he said, but Nolan wasn't talking. Either he'd made the eavesdropping call early, or Slater was running late. Hopefully the kid wasn't getting nervous, wasn't going to blow it.

Walking into the lobby, Slater hustled back to the elevators. The uniformed guard at the desk, absorbed in the blue glow of a screen, didn't even glance up at him. In his earpiece, Slater heard Nolan speaking.

"Mr. Hart will be right with you. Would you like to have a seat?"

Fainter but in her confident entitled tone, Grace said, "I'm not accustomed to being kept waiting."

"I'm sure it won't be long," Nolan said.

The sound cut out for a few seconds on the elevator ride up, but the call stayed connected, and Slater could still hear background noise when he stepped off. Hustling past Abner's front door, he went around the corner and stopped in the hall-way, his back to the wall. Standing here, he was far enough from Abner's door that it wouldn't look like he was eavesdropping.

In his earpiece came the sound of a door opening, and then Abner's nasal whine.

"Mrs. Higgins. Won't you come in?"

"It's Ms.," Grace said, in her affected formal tone.

"Of course."

As Slater waited, he heard muffled activity, then porcelain, like a cup landing on a saucer, and after that, the sound of a door opening. But that wasn't in his earpiece, it was here—farther down the hall. Quickly pulling out his phone, he studied the screen intently as a woman in a gray suit stepped out and walked past. In the periph-ery Slater saw her glance at him, but she seemed unconcerned at his presence.

She disappeared around the corner, and a moment later he heard the faint *ding* of one of the elevators arriving.

Tucking his phone away, he took a deep breath, then closed his eyes, listening intently. The sound of a door opening, Abner very faintly saying, "Here's my assistant. Can I offer you cof-fee?" The door closing, half a minute of silence, and then the door opening again. That should be Nolan, on his way out.

Moments later, at the corner of the hallway, Nolan appeared, wearing a yellow necktie with a gray satin shirt, and gave him a thumbs-up, then just stood there. Slater raised his eyebrows and jabbed a finger toward the elevators, and Nolan disappeared.

In his earpiece the outer office was silent, and Slater closed his eyes again, focusing on it. The elevator dinged, but that was just Nolan going down. A minute later came the clatter of activity and shouting and confusion, making Slater's heart pound.

The sound of the inner door opening, and then Grace's voice, loud and insistent.

"I said chest pains. All along this side, like my ribs are being crushed."

"Perhaps if you sat down," Abner said.

"Ooh, it's horrible," Grace said. "What did you put in that coffee? It tasted so strange. It made my lips go numb."

"There was nothing in the coffee," Abner said. "I'm going to call an ambulance."

Listening for the inner door to close, Slater couldn't hear it, but it must have happened.

"Take my arm," Grace insisted. "Help me. I'm feeling faint."

Stepping over to Abner's back door, Slater gave it a gentle tug, and it opened easily, revealing a strip of duct tape over the latch. He took a breath. Good job, Nolan. The door to the front office had closed itself, and Slater hustled over to it, carefully twisting the deadbolt. Abner had the key, of course, but if he decided to come back, that would slow him down, give Slater time to bail.

On the edge of Abner's desk was a dainty china saucer in a red rose pattern, and on the floor beneath it, the matching cup, unbroken but with a dark stain on the carpet around it—Grace had spilled her coffee. Glancing at the absurd red sausage-horse painting, spotlighted behind the desk, Slater went to the file cabinets at the side of the office.

"I can't understand where my assistant is," Abner's voice said in his ear. "I have to call someone."

"No—stay with me," Grace pleaded. "Hold my arm."

"Ms. Higgins, you're hurting me."

Slater pulled on the top drawer of the cabinet, but it was locked, and so was the next one.

"Damn it," he said under his breath. Who would do that—lock the cabinets in a room where you're the only one with a key? Abner must have plenty to hide.

Across the room, a tray with another rose-patterned china cup and saucer and an untouched plate of biscotti sat on the credenza. It didn't have a lock on it, but when Slater slid it open, there was no paperwork inside, only lowball glasses and a pair of bottles—expensive-looking scotch, like at Marisol's. He slid it shut. Maybe it was just as well—rifling through paper would take time. His plan had been to photograph anything suspicious and sort it all out later, but even that would take longer than he had, based on the pace of the crisis unfolding in the next room.

"Maybe I can stand," Grace said in his earpiece. "You have to help me. Come back here and help me."

Slater froze, listening for Abner trying to get in. But Grace must have drawn him back.

"The room's going dark," she cried. "Please, just take my arm."

Slater went to Abner's desk, devoid of paper but with his laptop sitting on it. He knew he was running out of time, and didn't pause to look in the desk drawers, instead pulling open the laptop. The screen flickered to life. It was password-protected, as expected. Slater felt in his pocket for the USB chip. Had he lost it? Digging in his other pockets, he felt his heart pounding. Had he inadvertently dropped it when he was paying the taco guy?

"I need an ambulance to the Durham Building," Abner's voice said. "There's an elderly woman having a heart attack."

That hadn't been part of the plan, letting him

do that. Grace was supposed to keep him away from the phone. Finally Slater found the drive, caught in the seam at the bottom of his pocket. Folding the laptop closed and quickly checking it for ports, he thought about Abner. The guy was probably right-handed, so he was less likely to use the ones on the left side. Pressing the drive in with his fingernail, he felt it softly click into place. So tiny that it was actually recessed inside the port, you'd need a hook to dig it out. But anyone trying to use the port would just assume the plastic housing had dislodged, or some internal component had been displaced. Things like that happened all the time. Abner wouldn't bother to try to fix it either, as there were other ports. And now, if things worked out, the next time Abner logged in, Slater would have access to his stuff.

"Don't leave me," Grace pleaded, her tone sharp. "This may be my last hour on earth."

Stepping over to the padded door to the outer office, Slater gently twisted the bolt open, then went to the door into the hall, peeling off Nolan's duct tape and gently closing it behind him, taking a breath when he heard it latch.

No one was in the hall, and he rolled the tape into a little ball and walked toward the elevators.

"Try to relax," Abner was saying in his earpiece. "The paramedics are on their way."

On the way down to the lobby, the elevator

stopped three times to let other people board, and the call cut out. He'd lost his ear on Grace.

As the doors opened and he stepped into the marbled lobby, the paramedics were on their way in from the street, three of them, in their dark-blue uniforms, one carrying a narrow yellow stretcher. That was fast. Hopefully Grace could handle them—it might be harder to fool someone who knew what a heart attack really looked like, and he didn't want her to get waylaid at an ER for the rest of the day.

Standing at the side of the lobby with a handful of curious office drones, Slater watched as the paramedics boarded an elevator, then wandered over to the building's front entrance. An ambulance was parked outside, the light bar flickering red and white. The lobby cleared out once the paramedics were gone. Not sure whether to leave or wait to see how it would play out, he looked at the security guard. The guy was talking quietly on his desk phone, not concerned about Slater.

Then one of the elevators opened, and Grace stepped out, smiling when she caught sight of him. With a nod, she gestured to the street. She was right—they didn't want to be seen talking in the lobby.

Heading out to the sidewalk, past the flashing ambulance, its engine idling noisily, he walked down the block and across the side street, ditching the sticky ball of duct tape when he passed a trash can. Just past the corner he waited near a fruit seller's cart, hoping to blend in with the handful of people buying cups of watermelon and cantaloupe for lunch.

Grace walked up, and Slater scanned the route behind her, making sure no one had followed.

"Your timing is impeccable," he said quietly. "You just missed the paramedics."

"I had a miraculous recovery," she said, still speaking in her formal voice, and Slater led her to his car.

Once he'd opened the door for her, he climbed in himself, checking the street again to make sure they hadn't been made. The ambulance was still parked in front of the Durham Building.

"You got in?" Grace asked.

"I did," Slater said, checking the side mirror and pulling into the traffic. "I heard some of your performance. I wish I could have seen it."

"Abner seemed quite worried that I was going to die in his office. He kept trying to get me to stand up. I kept him close to me for as long as I could, but he had his cell phone on him, so he was able to call the ambulance. I gave it a few more minutes and then had him help me up. He was thrilled when I was able to stand."

"So he bought it?"

"Completely," she said. "He was so relieved

that I wanted to leave."

"You, my dear, are a legend."

Grace laughed. "I'm just glad I timed it right. Those ambulance jockeys must have been right nearby."

FOURTEEN

———

fter he pulled the Thunderbird into his garage and waited for the door to roll down, he rode up in the little elevator with Grace.

Unlocking her apartment, she said, "Come in and I'll give you the ice."

The jewelry boxes were waiting on her dining table, and she pulled off the earrings and the bracelet, taking a last longing look at the swan pin before boxing it and handing the bag to Slater.

"So did you find what you were looking for?" she asked, finally lapsing into her regular voice.

"I won't know for a while. Thanks for your help."

"It felt like the old days," she said, and walked him to the door.

In his own apartment, Slater put on a clean shirt—with the pressure of skulking around Abner's office, the one he'd been wearing was soaked with sweat.

Downstairs again, he backed into the alley and drove to the Jewelry District, parking near Vahan's storefront. He was behind his counter, finishing up a sale with a woman who was dressed for an office job, and Slater waited until he handed her a black bag, just like the one he was carrying. She walked past Slater on her way out, a smile on her face.

"You know how to make your customers happy," Slater said.

Vahan shrugged. "It's a gift."

Slater set the bag on the counter.

"Done already?" Vahan said. "Did your lady like the pieces?"

"You have to check them. Make sure it's all there."

He reached into the bag and took out the boxes, putting the pin back into its case, setting the bracelet in its tray, and then looking closely at one of the earrings.

"There's a stone missing."

"What?" Slater snapped.

Vahan guffawed, his head tilting back, showing his gummy smile. "I'm just messing with you."

"Not funny," Slater said. "If everything is

intact, we're done. Tear up that invoice."

"If you have a minute," Vahan said, "I want to show you something in the back."

"No," Slater said firmly. "Say hello to your wife."

Vahan looked pained, and groaned as Slater turned to walk away. "You're killing me, Slater."

Most of the neighborhood was already in long shadows as he drove to his office, occasional glimpses of the low sun flickering between the buildings. Slater waved to the parking attendant and walked across the street. The day laborers had dispersed but the factories were still humming.

The office was dark, and doing a quick visual sweep, he saw that there was no sign Max had been in lately. Pulling out his phone, he checked the location of Max's phone. Unlike the hidden one he used to keep tabs on Conrad, he and Max had agreed to keep track of each other. The map in the tracking app showed a green dot in Highland Park, moving north on the 110. Max was in a vehicle. His girlfriend lived out that way, so it felt legit. He wouldn't bother to check in with him. The agreement was that they'd only come after each other if one of them were kidnapped or in the hoosegow.

At his desk he woke his computer and pulled up the interface for the Russian software. Abner's laptop was already visible. Checking the activity log, it had connected at 13:42. That was when he'd been in Abner's office. It meant the laptop was powered on and accessible even when it was closed, so it didn't matter whether Abner opened it. A smile spread across his face. Svetlana's tech was working flawlessly. All the effort had been worth it.

The USB drive gave him access to the device, although he couldn't see what Abner was doing or run any of the software. But he could see all the files. Clicking through the folders, he soon found what seemed to be work stuff—dozens of spreadsheets separated into subfolders. Some bore names that corresponded to the client list Andy had collated, including the Church of the Early Bright.

He'd make a copy of everything in Abner's work folders, Slater decided. Svetlana had explained that it might slow the device's performance for a few minutes, and take up more internet bandwidth, but most people didn't notice things like that, and Abner might not even be using it right now. It took several minutes to copy everything, slowed by the data's circuitous route through an anonymizing server in the motherland.

Once the transfer had finished, Slater checked that everything was there, clicking open a spreadsheet to make sure it wasn't corrupted, then another. Satisfied, he went back to the web page with the interface and clicked on a button labeled KILL. A bubble popped up with a skull-and-crossbones graphic, asking "Permanent disable of device?" Slater clicked on YES, and a moment later the link to Abner's laptop disappeared, replaced with "No connected device."

The software on the tiny drive had been erased, and if anyone ever bothered to pry it out, it would look like nothing more than a blank malfunctioning storage drive.

Before he got into looking at Abner's files in depth, he checked the time. Nolan would be leaving the office soon. He pulled up his contact list and dialed his cell.

When Nolan answered, Slater said, "You did great today."

"Did you find out what that guy was up to?"

That guy. He meant Abner, but he couldn't talk frankly because he was still at work, with Abner's security camera monitoring his office.

"Not yet, but I got what I needed. Is Abner still there?"

"My sources say no."

"Are you going to be around for a few minutes?"

"I work until six."

"I'm going to drop by," Slater said. "Can you unplug the security camera before I get there?"

"That won't be a problem. See you then," Nolan said.

Slater got up and went into Max's office, where he pulled open his desk drawers, rooting around until he found a blank envelope. Back in his own office, he wrote Nolan's name on it in black marker, underlining it twice.

Squatting to open the safe, he wondered how much he should pay him. They'd agreed on two hundred more, but that didn't seem right. Slater pulled out seven C-notes, then noted it on the cash envelope and locked the safe again. That made an even grand, plus the shoes.

Maybe overpaying him was rewarding the unethical behavior, Slater thought, as he tucked the bills into the envelope. Maybe he was pushing him farther down the path toward becoming a lowlife. But Nolan had earned it, and he could use the money. It was done, the envelope was sealed, and Slater pushed the doubt and the twinge of guilt out of his mind.

Stuffing the envelope into his pocket, he locked up the office and headed down to his car. Traffic was heavy, and it took a while to get to the Durham Building, but at least there was parking on the side street.

The guard at the desk in the lobby gave Slater the once-over as he strode past, and Slater nodded in acknowledgment. Upstairs at Abner's office, he rapped on the door and then pushed it open.

"The camera's off," Nolan said, twisting his

chair toward Slater as he came in.

"Good work." Slater glanced at the camera to make sure the green indicator below the lens was dead, then stood in front of his desk. "So what happened when you came back from your break?"

"I saw the paramedics in the lobby," Nolan said. "They were leaving without a patient. When I got up here, the client was gone, and Abner was totally stressed out. He grilled me—'How did that woman make that appointment?' and then he made me clean up the spilled coffee in his office. Your friend told him it tasted weird, and he wanted to know what I'd done differently."

"What did you say?"

"I told him the coffee was the same as always. He knew it was, because he drank it too."

"What did you tell him about the appointment?"

"That I didn't know anything about it—I'd never seen her before, and I didn't take the call."

"Excellent," Slater said, grinning at him. "Do you think he suspected anything?"

"I don't think so. He was kind of shaken up, but he had another meeting at 3:30, and that was routine, coffee and all. I didn't get a chance to check the door to the hall—did you remember the tape?"

"I peeled it off and ditched it in a trash can on Wilshire Boulevard. There's no evidence that anything ever happened, so you can forget all about it. Was your phone where you left it?"

"I covered it with a napkin beside the keyboard," Nolan said, glancing at his desktop. "I don't think anyone messed with it."

"You're a natural," Slater said, and pulled the cash envelope from his hip pocket. "This is the rest of what I owe you."

"Thanks," Nolan said, taking it and grinning when he saw his name written on the front. He pulled his backpack from under the desk and tucked the envelope into it.

"One other thing," Slater said, resting his hands on his hips. "I left a monitoring device here when we opened the ceiling. I need to get it back."

Nolan frowned. "You bugged my office?"

"I didn't know your role here. I thought you might have been as corrupt as Abner. Besides, Big Brother already has a constant eye on you."

"True," Nolan said, glancing up at the security camera. "So you put it in the ceiling? Did you bring a ladder?"

"I think I can reach it if I use one of the guest chairs," Slater said, and went to the side of the room, picking one up and carrying it to Nolan's desk. Nolan got up and rolled his desk chair out of the way.

Slater climbed on the chair and then carefully stepped onto the arms, gingerly getting his balance, and then looked up. The ceiling tile was just within reach, and he pushed it up, dislodging it, and then pulled the pencil camera out of the dusty fibrous material. When he reached for the battery pack, it slipped off the metal framework and dropped, whipping the camera with it, and landed on the chair mat with a loud *crack*. Slater managed to maintain his balance, not looking down but bracing himself on the ceiling frame.

"Careful," Nolan admonished, stepping closer to examine the camera. "It doesn't look like it broke. That's the thing you told me was a leak detector. It's huge."

"It's mostly battery," Slater said, and manipulated the ceiling tile back into place, then hopped off the chair.

"The stick part is the mike?"

"That's right." If he hadn't figured out it was a camera, Slater wasn't about to enlighten him. An audio bug seemed a lot less invasive.

While Slater moved the chair back, Nolan found a plastic grocery bag in the bottom drawer of his desk and put the camera in it.

"I'm about ready to head out," Nolan said. "Do you want to go get dinner or something?"

Slater took the shopping bag. "Yeah, about that. I won't be able to see you for a while."

"Are you giving me the brush-off?" Nolan said, his brow furrowing. "You got what you wanted, so now it's *Adiós?*"

"No, man. I just don't think we should get too close."

"And you get to decide that unilaterally."

"Listen to me," Slater said intently. "I'm not good for people. You saw today the kind of stuff I have to do. I don't want to drag you into that cesspool."

Nolan eyed him for a moment before he spoke. "Am I going to see you again?"

"Of course—you and Chino are going to invite me over for beers when you shack up together."

Nolan stepped toward him and pulled him into a tight hug. Slater kissed his neck and pulled away.

"Don't forget to plug the security camera in," Slater said before he left.

A clean break, Slater thought, riding down in the elevator. That was merciful, and sensible. Still, he felt bad about corrupting the kid, paying him to violate Abner's trust. Nolan had been open to it, though, so maybe he was already on that path. In any case, he was done making trouble for Nolan.

———◆———

Back in his own office, on his computer, he opened the jumble of folders with Abner's spreadsheets, clicking them open one after another, trying to parse the information they contained. There were some other documents too: letters, bank statements, filled-in tax forms. Even though he could understand all the words, all the titles and the line items in the spreadsheets, in aggregate it made no sense.

What had Andy told him? "It's OK to ask for help." He hadn't been talking about accounting, but Slater definitely needed help with this.

Again raiding Max's desk, he found an unused flash drive and plugged it in, copying all of Abner's files, then stuffed the drive into his pants. He texted Andy:

Do you have some time for me?

Slater had locked up and was on his way to the elevator when the reply came:

Always, petal.

That made him chuckle, and he was still grinning when he stepped out onto the dark street.

Slater parked in the lot next to Andy's building, paying the attendant the flat evening rate. Andy was in his T-shirt and boxers when he opened the door, and flashed a smile.

Following him in, he saw that all three of his computer monitors were lit up, with columns of numbers and a set of squiggly line graphs stacked at one side.

"What are you working on?" Slater asked.

"Just some data analysis."

"Can you look at something for me? I managed to copy a bunch of the accountant's work files—mostly spreadsheets."

"I could," Andy said, easing into his desk chair and eyeing Slater, "but I don't think I could decipher his accounting any better than you. Plus I'd have to … air-gap my computer, and that's a lot of work."

Slater put his hands on his hips. "What does that mean?"

"Your accountant might have tracking software in his files, to tell him whether they've been … copied or opened by someone else. An air-gapped computer isn't connected to the internet, so if that software exists, it can't report to him."

"Can't you just unplug your internet while you do it?" Slater said.

"The issue persists afterward. Even if you delete his files, they might leave something behind that will make the report once the machine is online again."

"Damn it," Slater snapped.

"Did you already open them?"

"On my computer at work."

"This guy isn't a bigshot, right?" Andy said. "He's just a small-time crook?"

"I think so."

"So it's unlikely he'd have a system like that in place. It's not off-the-shelf technology, and it takes a lot of work to set up."

"I'm pretty sure there's dirt in those files, so even if he finds out I've seen them, he's not going to rat me out to the cops."

"You don't call the cops when your dealer rips you off," Andy said, raising his eyebrows.

Slater chuckled. "Good analogy. He's also not part of a syndicate. He won't be sending the muscle after me."

"I'm still not going to look at the stuff."

"I get it," Slater said.

"Next time, buy a used computer for a hundred bucks and disconnect it from everything. After you've looked at the files, open it up and destroy the drive."

"I wish I'd thought of that."

"So do you want me to … rock your world?"

"Can we just chill?"

"Hell, yeah," Andy said, and got up, moving to his bed.

Slater kicked off his boots and climbed on with him, leaning back against the pillows. Andy put an arm around his waist, shifting closer, and rested his head on Slater's chest.

"I can hear your heart beating," Andy said softly, and they lay like that for a while, comfortable, quiet, connected.

Eventually Andy shifted position, and Slater saw that he had a raging hard-on tenting his boxers. Slater couldn't just ignore it, so he pulled it out and spent a minute jerking him off, their mouths locked together, until Andy thrashed and yelped as he climaxed.

If he thought Slater spent too much time on sex, this one was on Andy—Slater didn't need to hook up every night, but Andy got wood just from the physical proximity. Who was the real addict? Slater was in control of his sex life, had it organized—even more than the drinking.

———•———

Waking later, it was dark, and Andy was naked, his eyes closed, his breathing regular. Slater sat up and checked his phone. It was after midnight.

"Stay," Andy said softly, turning toward him.

"I have to go."

"You're cutting back, right? There's a bottle in the cupboard by the microwave. Drink what you want and come back to bed."

Slater got up to check. The room was cold, even though he still had his jeans on. Not turning on the room lights, he was able to see well enough by the ambient glow of the metropolis outside the big windows. Opening the cupboard and scanning its contents, he found a half-gallon bottle of bourbon, a better brand than what he got for himself. Andy must think he was a total lush if he'd bought a handle for him.

This would be a lot easier than driving to his apartment, he decided, and pulled it out, then cracked the seal, pouring an inch and a half into a glass. Replacing the bottle in the cupboard, he slammed the bourbon, wincing at the burn, and went back to the bed.

"Finished already?" Andy said, sleep in his voice.

"You think I'm a drunk."

"That's not what I said."

Slater slid off his pants and climbed in. Andy curled toward him and wrapped his arm around Slater's belly, telegraphing his rhythmic random movements, dampened now by sleep. It felt warm, and familiar, and right. Slater closed his eyes and leaned into him.

FIFTEEN

Andy was at his desk when Slater woke. It took him a moment to remember why he was here, and he watched Andy for a while, sitting there gazing at his screens, wearing the black plastic gauntlets that somehow compensated for the fine motor control he lacked so that he could manipulate the computer.

Finally Andy turned to him. "You're awake."

Slater just smiled at him and stretched.

"Do you want coffee?"

"I'll get it," Slater said, but didn't move.

"I feel like I'm being observed."

"Only in admiration," Slater said. "Not scientific scrutiny."

Andy turned back to his screen for a minute, then eyed Slater again.

"I could use a refill," he said firmly.

Slater hadn't meant to unnerve him. Rolling out of bed, he poured himself a coffee, then took the pot to Andy's desk and filled his cup.

Andy murmured "Thanks" and then ignored him. Slater grabbed his phone and sat in the easy chair under the windows. He found O'Dowd's number in his contacts and dialed.

When she picked up, he asked, "Do you have time for me today?"

"Have you finished itemizing your expenses?"

"I'm still working on that. I need your assessment of some documents. It's billable work."

"Sure," she said. "I'm in my office."

After he got dressed, he kissed Andy goodbye, then went down to his car, briefly arguing with the attendant over how much more he should pay for having left it there overnight.

O'Dowd's office was in Westwood, and his navigation app sent him on the 10. It wasn't congested this long after the morning commute, and half an hour later he pulled into the garage under her office tower.

He never would have thought of what Andy had laid out, that the files themselves might have monitoring or tracking built into them. It meant there was a chance he was putting O'Dowd at risk by showing her Abner's stuff. More likely, though, Abner wasn't tech-savvy enough to have organized something like that. Svetlana's little drive had easily broken into his laptop, and he seemed far more concerned with presenting the appearance of wealth than with worrying about security.

Slater had never been here, and it took him a minute to find O'Dowd's office, double-checking the suite number on his phone before he knocked, as her name wasn't on the door.

"Come in," she called to him, and he was glad he'd knocked first—her office was just the one room, and when he opened the door, he was standing in front of her cluttered desk. Paperwork covered every surface, stacked deep, with a constellation of fluorescent-colored sticky notes protruding all around from the folders and binders and books. O'Dowd was in her forties, her spiky African hair pulled up in a scarf, a baggy gray sweater hanging off her shoulders, exposing black bra straps. Clearly she was dressed for a work day, not for meeting people.

"You look busy," Slater said.

Smiling at him and leaning back in her chair, she said, "I'm always busy. It'll get worse in the New Year, though, in the run-up to tax time." She waved at the chair in front of her desk. "Move that stuff and sit down. What do you need me to look at?"

Slater lifted a stack of folders from the chair

and set them on top of others on the desk, then sat. "One of the reasons Max and I hired you was for your discretion," he said.

O'Dowd raised an eyebrow. "You and Max hired me to make your cash income look as legit as possible."

"Right," Slater said, and nodded. "I want you to look at some paperwork, but you can't ask how I got it, and you can't tell anyone about it."

O'Dowd winced and held up a palm. "You're new at this, so I'm not going to get offended. To be absolutely clear: I work for you, and nothing you say or show me will leave this room."

"Is that a lawyer thing?" Slater said. "You have to do things that way?"

"It's a me thing," she said. "Two people you should never lie to are your doctor and your lawyer."

"That sounds really wise."

"So show me what you've got, and don't waste my time by dancing around it."

Slater rose and pulled the flash drive out of his pants, handing it across the forest of paper on her desk.

"These are from an accountant," he said. "The folders have the names of his various clients. I don't care about their assets or what they're doing, but I need insight into the accountant's own assets—what he might be hiding from his wife. He owns a bar out of town, and I'm pretty sure he's using it to launder cash."

"I'm not a forensic accountant," she said, frowning at him.

"What does that mean?"

"It's a specialized skill—someone who can figure out what people have done by looking at their financial records. But if you give me a couple of days, I can have a look."

"It's kind of urgent," Slater said.

"You really don't know how lawyers work."

"Max said you weren't that kind of lawyer. I can pay you a premium if you do it now."

O'Dowd sighed. "Let's see what you've got," she said, and spun her chair around to her computer, leaning down to connect the flash drive.

Slater watched as she started opening spreadsheets, scanning and quickly clicking from one to the next.

"A lot of this is working files," she said, still looking at her screen. "Not stuff you'd show the clients."

"Does it give you any insights?"

She turned to Slater. "Why don't you go across the street and get a coffee? Come back in an hour or so and I'll let you know what I'm seeing."

"All right," Slater said, and stood up. He was hesitant to leave her alone with the drive, but Max had looked into her, and if Max said O'Dowd was the one, he had to believe he could trust her.

"I'm obviously not going to invoice you for this," she said, "so bring six hundred in cash when you come back."

"Can we talk about that?" Slater said. "It doesn't seem like all that much work."

"You've blown a huge hole in my workday, Slater. It's not negotiable."

"Six hundred it is," he said, and chuckled. Closing the door behind him, he headed across the street. He had that much cash in his pants, and the fact that she'd named a price meant she was on board, that she'd do the work. Maybe Max was right—she was the right person to do their accounting.

Across Wilshire Boulevard was the retail neighborhood fronting UCLA, and Slater walked the streets for a while, finally stopping at a noodle restaurant. The joint was busy, the crowd young, several of them in medical scrubs.

After he'd downed a bowl of noodles he found a coffeehouse and sat in a dark corner, sipping a soy latte. The dead-ass classical music filling the space was out of sync with the energetic youthful neighborhood, but maybe it discouraged loitering. Eventually it started to grate, and Slater checked the time. It had been long enough.

The noise of the traffic was a relief, once he stepped outside, and he headed back to O'Dowd's office, where he knocked and pushed the door open.

O'Dowd glanced up briefly and said, "One sec," then went back to her screen.

Slater sat and watched as she scrolled through a crowded spreadsheet, intermittently turning to a laptop beside it to type something into a less densely cluttered spreadsheet. She spent some time on the laptop, intently focused, oblivious to Slater's presence, not rattled by being observed, like Andy was. Finally she closed the sheets on the larger screen and then pulled out the flash drive, twisting around in her chair and handing it to him.

"This guy has chutzpah," she said, slumping back and rubbing her eyes.

"He's spinning the numbers for the tax man?"

She shook her head. "It's not about taxes. I know how to spin numbers, but I'd never do what he's doing. He's skimming from his clients."

"Interesting," Slater said, shifting forward. "A lot?"

"It's hard to tell. I don't have all the information. If he were doing my books, though, it's enough that I hope I'd notice."

"He's doing that to all his clients?"

"I only went through two of them," O'Dowd said. "The ones with the biggest numbers. But yeah, he's running the same scam on both."

"Where's the money going?"

She threw up her hands. "Who knows? I can't tell from what's here, but it's more than you could funnel through a bar, unless it was a really big one. Are you in business with this guy?"

"I'm investigating him."

O'Dowd watched him for a moment before she spoke, her eyes tired. "Did you ever hear of the Atomic Casino in Vegas?"

"Never."

"It was built in the 1950s, when Vegas was booming, and they imploded it in the 1990s to replace it with something bigger. The explosives all went off, but the building wouldn't go down. Eventually they figured out that the guy who built it used twice as much steel as he needed. He was building it for gangsters, and he was afraid of what they'd do to him if there were any structural problems, or if it fell down."

"So what happened?" Slater said.

"I think they got it knocked down eventually. The point is, you don't mess with gangsters."

"You recognized the client names."

"They're not all gangsters," she said intently, "but these are scary people. Drug industry, religious nuts, organized crime."

"When you meet the guy, he's nothing like his clients," Slater said. "He's a milquetoast."

"That's basically the template for accountants."

"Do you think he's taking too big a risk?"

"He can't be unaware of who his clients are," she said, "and what they're capable of."

"I know he is," Slater said, remembering the conversation Abner had with the churchman in the bar at the Baltimore.

"All I can say is that I specialize in creative accounting, but I'd never do what he's doing."

Slater rose and pulled out his wad of cash, then peeled off the C-notes, folded them lengthwise, and set them on a pile of folders on her desk.

"I still need your itemized expenses," she said, eyeing him as she reached for the bills.

"It's on my desk. I'm almost done—I just have to press 'Send.'"

She chuckled at that and waved as he left.

———•———

The 10 was jammed, most likely, as his navigation app sent him on Wilshire all the way downtown. Braking in the stop-and-go traffic, he thought about Abner, and what he was going to tell Marisol. Abner was on the take, undeniably, but things weren't clear-cut. This is why he hated boy-girl stuff—it was always a freaking mess.

When he got to Koreatown, he passed the Durham Building and turned into a side street, parking at a meter. The guard in the marble-clad lobby ignored him as he went back toward the elevators. In Abner's office, the woman with the dark-rimmed glasses was on the reception desk. She frowned at the sight of him.

"Is he in?" Slater said, approaching her desk.

"Not for you."

Stepping past her, Slater went to the door into Abner's office and threw it open. Behind him the receptionist protested sharply, but here was Abner, seated behind his desk.

"What the fuck is this?" Abner demanded, scowling at him.

"I just need a minute," Slater said.

"So make an appointment. You can't just push your way in here."

"This is important."

Abner eyed him for a moment, calculating, then said, "Fine. One minute." He nodded to the receptionist in the doorway behind Slater, and she left them alone. Abner straightened up in his chair, but it didn't improve his stature; his frame was built to look like he was slouching.

"What's the big emergency, cowboy?" he said. "Did Marisol decide not to pay you?"

"What's with the painting?" Slater said, nodding to the wall behind Abner. "I can't decide if it's a Martian horse or a bleeding sausage on a tray of beets."

"That artwork is worth more than you'll earn in a decade," Abner said, holding his gaze.

"What's the artist's name?"

"Does it matter? You wouldn't know it."

"All this," Slater said, gesturing at the painting and at Abner, "just confirms what I know about the world, and how screwed up things are. It's startling to see what you have to do to keep it all going."

"Why are you here?" Abner demanded.

Slater stepped closer to his desk. "I'm not sure why I'm doing this, because I know you're crooked—"

"Hey," Abner snapped, his brow furrowing.

Holding up a palm, Slater said, "Just listen for a minute."

"You're working for Marisol. Why would I listen to you? Are you the one who told her about the Live Wire?"

Marisol had been quick to bring that up, Slater thought.

"Dolores said some insurance guy was snooping around out there on the weekend," Abner said. "Was that you?"

Slater eyed him for a moment. Had he really not figured that out? If Abner was that obtuse, he was in even more danger than he'd thought.

"Dude," Slater said, raising his voice. "What did I just say? You can get upset with me afterward."

Abner pressed his lips into a tight line and gestured for him to continue.

"I'm way more versed in that world than you

are—grifters and deadbeats and chiselers. Working for lowlifes doesn't mean that you can just do it too."

"I don't know what you're talking about," Abner said.

"You're skimming from some dangerous people. If they catch you, you're done for. Some hiker will find your remains in a shallow grave up in the Angeles National Forest."

"I'm not stealing from anybody," he said, frowning. "You're helping Marisol steal from me."

"I don't give a damn about your divorce," Slater said, and sighed. "I don't know what I'm doing here."

As Slater turned to leave, Abner rose. "Hold on," he said, and stepped toward him.

Slater tensed up and balled his fists. Was he going to have to teach this guy a lesson? But Abner wasn't threatening him, standing close and looking him in the eye.

"Are you sleeping with her?" he asked quietly.

"You asked me that once before. I don't sleep with women."

Abner moved closer, leaning in and meeting his mouth, wet and warm and passionate. Slater went with it, letting himself enjoy the intense connection. Abner put his hands on Slater's waist and pulled him closer. Through his suit pants Slater could feel his woody, unbound and insistent. He put a hand on Abner's cheek, soft and freshly shaved.

Maybe that's why he'd come here—he knew this peroxide poseur had some gay in him. Maybe Slater had a soft spot for him, and didn't want Abner to get himself killed. Eventually Slater pulled back.

"Would you sleep with me?" Abner said softly.

"I can't," Slater said.

"Because I have a wife?"

"And a girlfriend," Slater said pointedly.

Abner chuckled at that, moving closer again, pressing his cheek to Slater's ear.

Slater squeezed his arm. "Just tread carefully in your business dealings," he said gently, then pulled away.

Walking out, he ignored the receptionist and headed toward the elevators. He didn't care that the guy had a girlfriend. The issue was that Abner was a hand grenade with the pin pulled out. A clueless opportunistic grifter was way more dangerous than a calculated and seasoned grifter.

Back in his car, he texted Marisol:

Can I see you today?

Her response came as he was driving toward his apartment:

Come to the house. I'll be there after 7.

Once he was in his place, he pulled off his boots and stretched out on the sofa, shifting to get comfortable, then laced his hands behind his head. Through the grimy window he could see a strip of sky above the building across the street. Watching the daylight fading, almost imperceptibly, he thought about how he was going to wind things up with Marisol.

———◆———

At seven he went down to the garage, backing into the alley. The sun was long gone, and he flicked on his headlights for the drive to Los Feliz.

When he rang the bell at Marisol's obnoxious mansion, Randall, the redheaded driver, wearing a black turtleneck, pulled open the door. Before Slater could react, he threw a punch, catching Slater on the mouth. His head snapped back, and he tasted blood.

"What the fuck?" Slater demanded, running his tongue over his teeth.

"Now we're even," Randall said, stepping back.

"Fair enough," Slater said, rubbing his lower lip and glaring at him as he stepped inside.

Randall moved backward, a wary eye on Slater, but he wasn't wary enough. When he got within range, Slater lunged to sucker-punch him, hard, and Randall bent over, folding in on himself and sinking to his knees.

"Why do you make me do this to you?" Slater shouted, kicking him in the ribs.

"Stop it," Marisol shouted, trotting down the stairs. "You'll kill him."

Slater paused and looked at her, breathing hard. She must have been out somewhere, as she was in full makeup and wearing a dark-blue dress. Randall, a fetal ball at his feet, hands covering his face, just whimpered.

"He hit me first," Slater said. "What did I say about keeping your monkey on a leash?"

Marisol rolled her eyes and said flatly, "Men." Descending another few steps, she said loudly, "Randall, go to my room, and stay there."

Panting, Randall didn't acknowledge her, and Marisol gestured for Slater to follow her back up the stairs. She didn't seem overly alarmed about the beat-down.

In the lounge with the view of the little yard, floodlights still blazing, Marisol stepped behind the bar, pouring scotch into a pair of tumblers.

"Randall thinks he's a badass," she said, "but he's not."

"I'm aware of that. Are you sleeping with him?"

Marisol grinned. "Why would you ask that? I'm separated. I'm allowed to date. I wanted you to put out, remember?"

Watching her complete the task, he stepped

toward the bar to take one of the tumblers from her. On the bar top was a stack of coasters, a familiar white disk printed with LIVE WIRE, a red line running behind it and shooting sparks from its tip.

Slater picked up the top one. "You've been to Albuquerque."

"I have some new assets there," she said, raising her eyebrows. "Sit down."

In case Randall was stupid enough to try to go at it again, he took a chair with a view of the doorway. Marisol dropped onto the sofa and crossed her legs. She was barefoot, and all her toenails were painted red.

"How did you manage that?" Slater said, and sipped at the heady scotch.

"I told Abner that I'd explain the Live Wire to the tax people. He decided he'd cut me in on the place instead."

"So you're doing your own negotiating?" Slater said. "You're not going through the lawyers?"

"I can't really have an officer of the court involved in that kind of transaction."

"So you just needed me to do the research," Slater said, and sipped from his glass.

"Correct. You've got something more for me today?"

"It seems like you've already figured it out."

"Abner's game with his clients? The Live

Wire is proof of that," she said. "Did you find direct evidence that he's stealing from them? It would be extremely useful to negotiate a more equitable cut."

"It could also get him killed, knowing who his clients are."

Her eyes grew wide. "Do you think I'd blackmail my own husband?" She dropped her chin, her expression coy. "Slater, I'm a simple woman."

More like a dangerous woman, he thought. Shifting his leg, he could feel the thumb drive in his pants pocket, a hard little box with all that information, all that evidence, all that damning data.

"I don't have anything concrete," he said. "I heard rumors from some of his contacts."

"Like what?"

"I spoke to a guy who works at the Church of the Early Bright," Slater said, gesturing casually, thinking quickly. "He said he couldn't figure out why some of their revenue streams weren't more profitable. He wondered if Abner was being sloppy in keeping track of things."

"Are they going to confront him?" she asked, holding his gaze and absently swirling the contents of her glass.

"I doubt it. This guy just had a vague notion that something was amiss, and he wouldn't show me the paperwork."

"Well," she said, looking away, "You got me enough. Having the details on that bar is huge."

"And now you're in on it."

"Right." She grinned. "That means I don't have to kill him to get all his assets before the divorce."

"Were you planning that?" Slater said, holding her gaze.

"I thought I might get you to do it." Her brow furrowed. "Not in a way that would put you in prison, of course. I wouldn't do that to you."

"Of course you wouldn't," Slater said, mimicking her expression of concern.

If she were that blasé about icing her own husband, why would she hesitate to do that to Slater? The talk about how dangerous Abner was, that he was an unpredictable snake, and that he was armed—she'd planned to set him up all along.

Draining his glass, he paused to relish the burn and sat forward. "It sounds like you got what you need from me. We should settle up."

"Can you prepare an invoice?" she said, raising her eyebrows, channeling the ingenue once again.

"My business is like yours. It works better when nothing gets written down, and transactions are done in cash."

Marisol smiled. "It was worth a try. What do I owe you?"

Finally, he thought, relieved to hear that she wasn't going to try to chisel him too.

Walking in here, he'd planned to ask for six grand and settle for five. She'd lied to him—that wasn't unexpected; everyone did—but she'd admitted to manipulating him, and had planned to set him up, and that had to cost.

"Eight grand," he said.

"Sure." Marisol rose. "Give me a second."

Slater got up too and stood at the French doors, gazing out at the manzanita, the succulents, the scrubby poppies, stark and surreal in the blue-white floodlights.

When Marisol came back, she handed him a cash brick of hundreds. They were from a bank, still bound in a yellow band. Flipping through them, he saw they were new and sequential.

"This is a full rack," Slater said. "Am I going to be able to spend this?"

Marisol laughed. "It's clean money. Abner's specialty, remember? There's a little extra there to help keep your mouth shut."

"That's my specialty," Slater said. Waggling the bundle, he said pointedly, "This concludes our business."

"I might need you again one day," she said. "Can I call you?"

"Sure," he said simply, and walked toward the stairs, tucking the rack into his hip pocket, then trotting down to the front door.

"Give Randall a kiss good-night from me," Slater said, pulling open the front door.

Marisol laughed again. "He'll love that."

Nosing the Thunderbird down the dark narrow street, Slater felt lighter, the whole case lifting off his shoulders. He had to go downtown now and put this rack in the safe. Max would be happy to see all those new zeroes written on the accounting envelope, and they'd be able to make rent for a while.

Accelerating onto the 5, he matched the speed of the taillights in front. From the start Marisol had just used him to get dirt on Abner. That wasn't surprising, although he would have preferred the truth, not the innocent fawn routine. It actually made it easier not to turn over the details about Abner's grift. That would have given her much more leverage, and put Abner's life in more jeopardy than it already was. He felt a little bad for Abner, uncovering his secret bar so that Marisol could get her hooks into it. But he was on the take, so maybe he was getting what he deserved—Marisol was chiseling the chiseler.

Also from Dagmar Miura

That First Heady Burn

The first book in the Slater Ibáñez series sees Slater running surveillance on an injured tech worker and tangling with blackmailers, party girls, late-night hookups with a gamut of guys, and a lot of bourbon.

slater.dagmarmiura.com

The Mason Braithwaite Paranormal Mystery Series

No one is ever quite sure whether psychic investigator Mason gets results with actual psychic power or his more mundane flatfooting, but the disheveled redhead manages to resolve some intractable mysteries.

mason.dagmarmiura.com

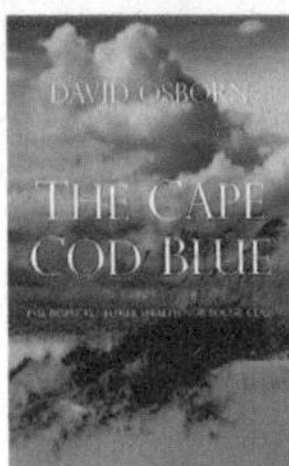

The Cape Cod Blue

The glittering, exalted world of art auctioning hides love, hate, and parricidal murder in a wealthy and socially prominent family when forgery of an anonymous Cape Cod painting is used to steal a world-famous portrait that's worth a fortune.

capecod.dagmarmiura.com

The Bone Bridge

Yarrott Benz, the 2016 Ippy Award winner for memoir, is forced to deal with extraordinary self-sacrifice in this harrowing account of teenage brothers, as different as night and day, trapped together in a dramatic medical dilemma.

bonebridge.dagmarmiura.com